SWAN SONG

JUDITH BLEVINS

SWAN SONG

A NOVEL

JUDITH BLEVINS

BRASS FROG BOOKWORKS™
Independent Publishers
Grand Junction, CO
www.BrassFrogBookworks.com

Published by BRASS FROG BOOKWORKS™ Independent Publishers
2695 Patterson Rd. Unit 2-#168 | Grand Junction, CO 81506 |909-239-0344 or 970-434-9361 |
www.BrassFrogBookworks.com

Brass Frog Bookworks™ is dedicated to excellence and integrity in the publishing industry. BFB was established on the belief in the power of language and the spiritual essence of human creativity. "In the beginning was the Word…" John 1:1

Book design copyright © 2014 by Brass Frog Bookworks™. All rights reserved
Interior Design: Laurie Goralka Design
Cover: J Leon - ClickConstruction

Address inquiries to:
Judith Blevins
Fountainhead Blvd. G-8
Grand Junction, CO 81505

Printed in the United States of America | First Printing 2014
Library of Congress Control Number: 2013958184
ISBN: 978-0-9899412-0-4

1. Fiction/Romance
2. Fiction/Crime
3. Fiction/Suspense

Other Titles by Judith Blevins

DOUBLE JEOPARDY - Love blows into Farmington like the searing desert wind when high school friends Nick and Jas are reunited after many long years. The spark between them is soon fanned into an inferno of passion. Grateful to have a second chance for happiness, they dream of a life together. But their private demons are too much. When Jas begins to doubt Nick, a force is ignited that will forever change the course of their lives. Jas has blood on her hands. Is she a cold-blooded murderer? Follow the intriguing events as they unfold and spiral wildly out of control then culminate in an incredible, unexpected conclusion.

ACKNOWLEDGMENTS

Special thanks to fellow fiction writer, Carroll Multz, for his support, editing skills, inspiration and advice. Without Carroll's encouragement and prodding, my novels would still be rattling around in my head.

To my publisher, Brass Frog Bookworks™ and my editors, Patti Hoff and Cindy Stein, I extend my gratitude for their expertise and guidance in helping me finalize *Swan Song*.

*Believe with all of your heart that you
will do what you were made to do.*
Orison Swett Marden

TABLE OF CONTENTS

Prologue. 1

CHAPTER 1
Life is Just a Bowl of Cherries 18

CHAPTER 2
No Guts, No Glory 24

CHAPTER 3
Nothing Ventured, Nothing Gained . . 32

CHAPTER 4
What You Don't Know Won't Hurt You . 51

CHAPTER 5
Have Your Cake and Eat it Too 68

CHAPTER 6
All's Fair in Love and War 78

CHAPTER 7
Against the Middle. 95

CHAPTER 8
The Pen is Mightier than the Sword. .111

CHAPTER 9
Devil and the Deep Blue Sea 138

CHAPTER 10
Beauty is Only Skin Deep. 147

CHAPTER 11
Flirting With Disaster. 157

CHAPTER 12
The Bigger They Are, the Harder
    They Fall. 174

CHAPTER 13
The World, the Flesh and the Devil . .181

CHAPTER 14
An Eye for an Eye 205

CHAPTER 15
What Goes Around 234

Epilogue 248

"DAMN YANKEES!" Vern cursed as he switched off the radio. He had been listening to his favorite team as he sat sweltering in his Range Rover. *Bases loaded and Jepson strikes out?* Exasperated, he flopped his head back against the seat and stared out the windshield. Looking up, he noticed the man he had been tailing, Senator Mark Langford, and the woman Langford had been seeing, Gabrielle LaTana, engaged in a struggle on her balcony. Vern grabbed his Nikon and zoomed in on the couple. He watched Gabrielle, screaming and crying, as she attempted to pull away from Langford's grasp. Vern snapped photographs in rapid succession.

Looking through the zoom lens, he saw Gabrielle jerk her arm free and stumble backwards. Langford rushed toward her with his arms outstretched. Suddenly turning, Gabrielle slammed into the balcony railing. Vern heard the scream and watched, as if in slow motion, Gabrielle topple over the railing, her arms wildly pin wheeling as she fell four stories to her death. Vern got it all on film. *Oh, my God, did that bastard just push her?*

After the initial shock, Vern looked up just in time to see Langford peering over the railing. He continued snapping shots as he watched

Langford's shoulders slump and saw him cover his face with both hands, as though trying to shut out the horror of it all. A moment later, Langford disappeared into the building.

Vern jumped out of his vehicle and joined the stunned crowd that gathered around the mangled, bleeding body. He positioned himself to watch the side exit believing Langford would try to sneak out undetected. His instincts proved correct. Vern leveled his camera and took several more shots of Langford slipping out of the stairwell door and slinking down the street. Vern watched as Langford stepped off the curb and hailed a taxi.

The NYPD arrived on the scene about the same time as the EMTs. Lead Detective Steve Carson elbowed his way through the crowd that had gathered and began barking orders to the uniforms.

"Establish a perimeter and move everyone back." Turning to the crowd, he shouted over the din, "Anyone here know what happened or the name of the victim?"

"I do." A middle-aged man stepped forward.

"Come over here, sir," Carson ordered. When the man approached, Carson asked, "Who is she?"

"Gabrielle LaTana." The man's voice shook. "She lived in this apartment building."

"How do you know her?"

"I manage these apartments," he answered with a sweep of his arm.

"What's your name?" Carson asked, jotting on his notepad.

"Jim. . .James Wilson."

"Do you live on the premises?"

"Yes, I live right there, apartment 101," Wilson nodded toward the balcony on the ground floor.

"What apartment did she live in?"

"She shared 401 with a roommate, Cynthia Sawyer."

Carson held up a finger as he dialed his cell phone. He called his fellow officer, Daniel Alexander, a twenty-year homicide veteran with the NYPD, who was also at the scene.

"Dan, the victim has been identified as Gabrielle LaTana, apartment number 401. Get the CSI team over here right away. I'm talking with the manager and will obtain a key." He looked at Wilson, who promptly removed a key from the large key ring hanging from his belt.

Detective Alexander pushed his way through the throng to where Carson was waiting.

"I'll join you as soon as I finish here," Carson said to Alexander.

"Roger that, Steve," Alexander replied.

Carson handed over the key, and Alexander headed for apartment 401.

Continuing his discussion with Wilson, Carson looked up. "Where's 401's balcony?"

"My place is right here. As you can see, the balconies are staggered," Wilson said. "201 is to the left of mine, 301 is directly above mine and 401, again, is to the left.

"Did you see what happened?"

"I saw her fall. I was out on my balcony coaxing Jinx, that's my calico, to come in when I heard the scream and saw Gabrielle tumble to her death. I'm the one who called 911. Do you think he pushed her?"

Carson jerked his head up and leveled his gaze on Wilson. Frowning and with his pen poised above his notepad, he asked, "What are you talking about? Did you see someone with her before she fell?" Carson looked up and scanned the face of the building. He scratched his head. "You really can't see onto her balcony from here. Why do you think someone may have pushed her?"

"I heard a ruckus right before she went over. I heard them arguing."

"Just exactly who did you hear arguing?"

"Gabrielle and her boyfriend. Why, that guy that came around regularly. Nice looking fellow, clean cut and always dressed to the nines."

"Do you know his name?"

"No."

"What were they arguing about?"

"Hard to say. She was screaming and sobbing, couldn't understand her. He was saying something like 'No, Gabrielle, calm down. Don't. . .' Then in the next instant, I saw her zoom past my place and hit the pavement right before my eyes. Right there." Wilson pointed to where she lay on the bloodstained walkway.

"Then what happened?"

"I called 911 right away, but I could tell she was a goner."

"You said this man came around often, but you don't know his name?"

"That's right." Wilson shrugged his shoulders. "I never actually met him. I just saw him in passing as I was cleaning the walk or mowing the lawn. He was always in a hurry to get inside the building."

"How often did he visit her?"

"Couple, maybe three times a week. Sometimes more."

"How'd he get here? Drive? Taxi. . . ?"

"Taxi."

"Did he always come alone?"

"He was always alone on the occasions I saw him."

"Can you describe him?"

"Sure. He's maybe six foot tall, weighs about 175, late thirties, early forties, dark hair, gray eyes, nice athletic build, broad shoulders."

"Would you recognize him if you saw him, say, in a lineup?"

"I think I would. I saw him often enough." A car alarm blared in the distance.

"What time did he arrive today?"

"It was two on the nose. The clock chimed and scared Jinx just when I almost had 'er."

"You called 911 at two-ten, so he was only there maybe ten minutes before she fell. What do you know about Gabrielle? Did you ever talk to her?"

"Just spoke to her casually now and then when I'd see her outside the apartment or when I had to fix something in their apartment. She was a nice girl. Worked at a spa over by the UN. She was good lookin' enough, that's for sure. Heard she won a beauty contest in Monaco."

"Did she seem depressed?" Carson raised his eyebrows.

"Not at all, she was always upbeat."

"Did the roommates get along?"

"Better than sisters."

I hope he means better than my sisters do. "Do you mean they were friends?"

"Absolutely, they were good friends."

"Did they have any other regular visitors that you know of?"

"Can't say. Cynthia was gone most of the time, and Gabrielle kept pretty much to herself. So, no. Not to my knowledge."

Carson examined his notes. "You've been very helpful. We may want to talk to you again, but this will do for now. We'll be in touch. If you think of anything, even if you don't think it is important, please contact me. Here's my card—call day or night."

"Sure thing, Detective Carson," Wilson said as he looked at the card before slipping it into the breast pocket of his shirt.

Carson left Wilson standing outside the apartment building and took the elevator to the fourth floor. The crime scene techs had already begun to sweep 401, and the coroner was removing the body from the scene.

"If this was a suicide, then so were all of Jack the Ripper's victims," Carson muttered to the officers within earshot. "For God's sake, it was middle of the day and she was wearing a pink negligée. This smacks more of a rendezvous that ended very badly for her." Carson flipped his notebook closed and took another look around. The crime scene techs were dusting for prints and gathering evidence, and Carson was just in their way. "I'm heading back uptown. All of you meet me back at the station when you're done here."

"Steve," Ramie Anson, a relative new comer to the 42nd, said as he dusted fingerprint powder on the kitchen counter, "somethin' you should know. . . ."

"What's that, Ramie?"

"Doorknob's wiped—both sides."

"No prints on the doorknob?"

"Not a single one."

"You're sure?"

"That's an insult. Of *course*, I'm sure."

"Didn't mean. . . Don't take it personal, that's just so strange. . . This is looking more and more like homicide."

"Yep, that's my take."

"That's just so strange—both sides," Carson said again and slapped Anson on the back in an attempt to soften what Anson no doubt had considered an insult. Then, rubbing his brow, Carson turned and asked Daniel Alexander, "Anyone got a lead on the roommate yet?"

"We have her name, Cynthia Sawyer. Found out from neighbors that Sawyer and the victim worked at *BellaDonna Beauty Spa*. It's located close to the UN. Neighbor also told us Sawyer attends night classes at NYU. She usually gets home from work around three. She's here for a couple of hours and then leaves for class. I'm going to intercept her in the lobby before she walks into this mess."

"Good plan. Catch her off guard so she doesn't have a chance to contrive a story. I don't need to tell you your job, but you know how anal I am."

Carson watched as Alexander rolled his eyes in acknowledgment. Carson ignored the gesture and continued, "Find out if the victim was depressed or appeared to be suicidal. Was she seeing anyone? Did she have any enemies? You know the drill, probably better than I."

"So true! Didn't I mentor you way back when?"

"Yep and now look at me. You did a fine job. I commend you! I'm on my way back uptown. I scheduled a meeting this afternoon with the team at 6:30. We should have the coroner's report by then. If you're not finished interviewing Sawyer, we'll wait for you."

"I'll call in if it looks like I'm running over. I want to be in on the ground floor."

"Good idea. I'll postpone until you get there—even if it means overtime."

Detective Daniel Alexander descended the stairs to the first floor, went out of the building, and took up a position on the concrete steps leading into the Brookline Apartments. He checked his watch, 2:53. *Sawyer should be along any minute now.* He looked toward the bus stop on the corner. Standing on the walkway with one foot on the second step, Alexander rested his right forearm on his thigh and was thumbing through his notes when the exhaust belched. The bus braked to a stop at the corner. Alexander straightened and watched as a pretty, young woman stepped from the bus. She walked toward the apartment building, obviously troubled upon seeing the police vehicles and the uniforms that were still on the scene. Alexander heard her ask an officer, "Excuse me, what happened here?" The officer had his back to Alexander so he couldn't hear the officer's reply but saw him turn and point in Alexander's direction.

Cynthia gathered her denim jacket across her chest and strode toward Alexander.

"I'm Cynthia Sawyer. I live here. What happened?"

"Come inside, Ms. Sawyer," Alexander beckoned as he led her up the steps.

The young woman's face grew pale. Her brow arched into a frown, and her head swiveled from side to side taking in the scene.

She grimaced at the wide crimson pool staining the walk and quickly looked away. The young woman looked like she might get sick. She squeezed her eyes shut and reopened them. "Has someone been hurt?"

"I'm sorry to have to inform you that your roommate, Gabrielle LaTana, fell from the balcony.

Cynthia clutched her chest as her breath escaped in a loud gasp. She leaned against the wall for support.

"She died instantly," the detective added as though this fact might bring some measure of comfort.

"I don't believe it! How could Gabrielle fall off the balcony? She never went out there. She was afraid of heights. You're joking, aren't you?"

Alexander knew Cynthia believed him—she was in denial. He took her hand and led her into the lobby. "Let's sit here. I need to talk to you."

A cry escaped from the depths of Cynthia's being, and she completely broke down. Sobs racked her body. Alexander put his arm around her shoulders and held her while she cried for her dead friend. After a few minutes, Cynthia straightened and pushed away from Alexander. Violently brushing tears from her cheeks, she said, "Tell me how it happened."

"That's what we're trying to piece together. You can help by answering a few questions."

"Okay. . . ," Cynthia said, sniffling into a crumpled tissue fished from her jacket pocket.

"Did Gabrielle seem depressed? I mean, we're not discounting suicide." Alexander flipped open his notepad and poised to write.

"No, not at all. In fact, I've never seen her happier."

"How's that?"

"There was someone special in her life, and she was head-over-heels. She looked forward to each day with hope and expectation."

"Who is this someone? Do you know his name?"

Cynthia gulped and looked down. "Why. . .why, no. She never told me his name, and I've never met him. He always came to see her when I was in class."

She's lying. I wonder who she is protecting. "How long had she been seeing him?" Alexander asked.

"A year or so."

"A year or so and she never mentioned his name?"

"Not to me. She was real secretive about their relationship."

"How long have you known Gabrielle?"

"Almost two years."

"I understand she's from Monaco. How did the two of you meet?"

"In fact, she was Miss Monaco a little over two years ago. That was way before we became friends. We worked together for a while, that's how we met."

H-m-m-m. She is certainly not giving up anything. My suspicious nature tells me this little girl knows much more than she's telling. "Where did you work together?"

"Actually at two different places. *Amazing You*, a defunct cosmetic retailer and more recently *BellaDonna*, a beauty salon and spa."

"What do you do there?"

"I'm a cosmetic consultant. Gabrielle was a manicurist." Another sob escaped followed by uncontrollable hiccups.

"Do you have anywhere you can stay the night? We're still investigating and you won't be allowed into your apartment until we're finished."

Cynthia slowly shook her head. "No. Not that I can think of. I can. . . ."

Jim Wilson, standing off to the side within earshot, interrupted, "Pardon me, I couldn't help overhearing you. I have an empty apartment here on the ground floor Cynthia can use until you complete your investigation."

"That's very kind of you, Mr. Wilson," Alexander looked at Cynthia.

She nodded, and after a brief pause asked, "Will I be allowed to get some personal items?"

Alexander rubbed his chin. It was against policy but, what the hell! "Sure, but I'll have to accompany you and inventory the items taken from the scene. . .er-r, premises."

"I understand." She turned and said, "Thank you, Mr. Wilson. That is very generous."

Wilson fumbled with his key ring again. Finally, finding the key, he removed it from the ring and handed it to Cynthia. "Apartment 102, just down the hall," he said and pointed. "It's one of the furnished units, so you should be comfortable. You can use it as long as you need. My wife will be home soon and she can help you get situated."

Alexander stood up and folded his notepad. "That's all for now, Cynthia. Let's go get the items you need from your apartment." Alexander looked at Wilson. "Where was your wife when this happened?"

"She works at a day care on the other side of town. She leaves at eight and gets home around four. She doesn't know about any of this yet."

"I see. Does she work tomorrow?"

"No, she works every other day. She job-shares with another woman. Works out well for both."

"I would like to interview her. Okay if I come by tomorrow, sometime in the morning?"

"Of course. We'll be expecting you."

✑

The crime scene investigators met in the conference room at the 42nd Precinct station house later that day. Carson had commandeered a whiteboard and had listed the evidence they had established to date. Five men were present: Lead Detective Steve Carson, Detectives Daniel Alexander, Charlie Sorenson, Pete Loftin and Ramie Anson.

"Here's what we know so far." Carson pointed to each item on the list. "One—Coroner's report lists cause of death as a fatal fall. Time of death is approximately 2:15 p.m. The only other mark on her body was bruising around her right wrist.

"Two—Interviews reveal no known enemies. General consensus was she was personable and people liked her. She was Miss Monaco two years earlier.

"Three—Roommate, Cynthia Sawyer, was devastated when she learned of Gabrielle's death. She knew Gabrielle was seeing someone but didn't know who it was and that she was always gone when the couple met. I'm convinced there's more to this than Cynthia is saying. I'm going to bring her in tomorrow for an in-depth interview. Perhaps a different environment, like the station house, will jog her memory. Dan, I want you to sit in with us since you've already talked to her."

Dan Alexander nodded.

"Four—The doorknob was wiped, both sides. Ramie is running other latent prints. We should have results in a few days.

"Five—Victim was dressed in a flimsy negligée and it was two in the afternoon. Jim Wilson, apartment manager, reported he heard the vic and an unknown male arguing on the balcony immediately before she fell. Wilson also said he saw a clean cut, nicely dressed male frequent the vic's apartment. We need to find out who Mr. Clean-Cut is—top priority.

"Charlie, Wilson's wife, is off work tomorrow. I want to have her interviewed. As we all know, women are much better at details than men are. If Clean-Cut visited as often as Wilson indicated, Alice could be a bottomless pit of information. Also, contact the others in the building and re-interview the neighbors. They may have remembered something overnight. Dan's sitting in with me on the Sawyer interview, so take Pete with you."

Carson looked down at his notes and back at the four men sitting around the conference table. "That's it for now. My gut tells me this is not a suicide. Good luck with your interviews. Meet back here tomorrow at four."

After Gabrielle LaTana's fall, Vern Simson hung around long enough to get pictures of Mark leaving the building. Vern had been a homicide detective with the NYPD for thirteen years before opening his own shop. During that time, he learned the art of obtaining quality photos. He was experienced enough to incorporate the newspaper stand that sported a neon with the date and changing time by the bus stop on the corner in most of his shots thus verifying the date the photos were taken. On the way back to his office, Vern stopped at Quick Pic to get his film developed. He didn't worry about having the content of his photos reported to the authorities; the kid who did the developing was his nephew.

"Hey, kid! Whasup? How's your old man?"

"Uncle Vern!" Jerry Simson said. "Long time no see. Where ya been?"

"Around. You know me, here today—back tomorrow. Seriously, how's your dad doing?"

"Better. The cancer is still in remission. You need to come around more often. He dotes on his little brother."

"I know. A phone call now-and-again just don't cut it. Tell Joe I'll be by Wednesday afternoon and to get the beer on ice. Say, Jerry, I've got some candid shots here. Develop them for me?"

"Sure. I'll do it now. Things are pretty slow."

"Swell. I'll go next door and get us a shake while you're developing."

"You're a life saver. Twenty minutes."

Vern reentered the photo shop just as Jerry was coming out of the darkroom.

"Pretty gruesome stuff. What happened?"

"Not sure. It was hard to tell from my vantage point. Right now, the place is swarming with cops. It should make the evening news. Here's your shake—chocolate if I remember. Right?"

"You do, and thank you," Jerry said, punching figures into the register. "Developing comes to eight fifty."

Vern gave Jerry a twenty. "Keep the change. See ya Wednesday," he said as he walked toward the entrance.

"Your visit will make Dad's day. He needs all the support he can get."

Feeling pretty much like a heel without a soul for ignoring his big brother, Vern promised himself he would do better.

Vern leafed through the photos before he left the parking lot. He was pleased with the quality of his shots. He drove to the Bronx where he rented office space and wheeled into his reserved parking slot.

Pausing in front of his office door, he swiped his jacket sleeve across the name painted on the frosted-glass window advertising *VERN SIMSON—PRIVATE INVESTIGATIONS. Sure beats the hell outta working for the PD, but I do miss the monthly trip to the bank.* Squatting in front of the door, Vern located the piece of thread he had placed between the door and the doorjamb when he left. It was undisturbed. He straightened and smiled. *Maybe it's Sam Spade corny but it works. Saved my life once.*

Satisfied no one was waiting to ambush him, Vern entered the office and tossed his Yankee's baseball cap toward the coat rack in the corner. The cap hit the wall and fluttered to the floor. One of these days I'm gonna nail it, Vern thought and flopped down in his worn leather chair. He took a bottle of bourbon from his bottom desk drawer and propped his feet on his beat-up wooden desk. Leaning back, he lit his favorite stogie and sipped his drink. He flipped through the photos once more. *I think Ms. Cash Cow Kara would be extremely interested in purchasing this set of photos. Screw the PD! Let 'em do their own investigating.*

CHAPTER 1

LIFE IS JUST A BOWL OF CHERRIES

Two years earlier.

KARA JERKED. She had dozed for most of the trip, but when she sensed a change in the rhythm of the plane's movement, she became wide awake. To her surprise, it was already twilight.

As the flight approached Kennedy International, Kara excitedly watched from her window seat as the plane descended. Liberty Island and the Statue of Liberty came into view below her before they slipped past.

Addressing the gentleman in the aisle seat, she said, "Look, we're flying over the Statue of Liberty. I've seen pictures of it, but nothing compares to the real thing. Can you see?" Kara pressed back against the seat to give her seatmate a better view out of the window.

"I've seen it numerous times. I fly this route often. By the way, I'm Senator Mark Langford at your service. And, you're. . .?"

"Kara, Kara Isabella."

"Happy to meet you Kara Isabella. What brings you to the States?"

"I'm beginning a new career as an interpreter with the Spanish Embassy at the UN."

"That's wonderful. I, too, have connections with the Spanish Embassy. I was appointed by the President to assist Spain in her economic recovery, and in that capacity, I'm required to make frequent visits to Spain. You'll like working with Ambassador Madrid and his staff. By the way, what happened to Lorraine, your predecessor?"

"She was called home. I don't know the circumstances."

"What a pity. I mean, I hope it isn't bad news. I spend many hours meeting with the ambassador, so you and I will no doubt be seeing a lot of each other."

"I've never met him personally but am looking forward to it." Kara remained fixed on the window. "I've heard many good things about him." She turned to face him. "Do you speak Spanish?"

"Only enough to get myself into trouble. You can believe what you've heard about Ambassador Madrid. I find him to be an extraordinary fellow and like him very much."

"Where are you from, Senator?"

"I hail from the great state of Indiana. Born there some thirty-six years ago. This is my second term in the Senate. Working with Spain has been a pleasure as well as an education. What part of Spain are you from?"

"Close to Madrid. My family has lived in the same place for over five hundred years."

"By same place, you mean the vicinity of Madrid?"

"No, I mean the same *residence*," Kara said, loving the effect she was having on the Senator as she toyed with him.

"So, you're telling me your home is over five hundred years old? Is it made of *stone*?" Mark teased.

"Most castles are made of stone."

"Well, now, Cinderella, is there a Prince Charming looming on the horizon?"

"You're making fun of me, aren't you?" Kara plucked the *Sky High* magazine from the seat pocket in front of her. "When you arrive at your destination, look up *Casa de Isabella* on the Internet. That's my family home and where I grew up," Kara replied, rapidly turning the magazine pages in a display of impatience at being challenged.

"I'm not making fun of you," Mark said somewhat apologetically. "I'm intrigued by Spanish culture—and by you. He leaned over and glanced out the porthole as the plane swung off the runway and taxied up to the gate. He glanced at Kara and smiled. There was a twinkle in his eyes. "Please forgive my ill-advised joking and say you will have dinner with me someday soon so I can make amends for my *faux pas.*"

Kara smiled and turned back to her magazine. "That sounds inviting. I'd like that."

Kara and Mark were seated in first class, so they were among the first to deplane. Being a Senator, Mark waltzed through customs. On his way to collect his luggage, he paused when he saw Kara waiting in line to clear customs.

"Wish I could do something to get you through quicker, but my power is severely limited in airports."

"That's all right. I'm rather enjoying the sights and sounds of New York. The chaos is even entertaining." Kara was never a patient person, but she didn't want Mark to see that side of her. She removed her jacket, draped it over her arm, and shifted from one foot to another as she placed her purse in the plastic container. "Thank you for your concern, but I'll be just fine. I think someone is waving at you over there."

Mark turned to look. "Oh, yes. That's Jonathan Logan. He works in the New York office. I'm spending the night at his residence. We have a meeting with the delegation tomorrow morning. No sense driving to DC and then back here for the meeting. Do you report for duty tomorrow?"

"I have a few days to get settled. My first day will be Monday, so perhaps I'll see you then."

"I'll make it a point." He waved an acknowledgment at Jonathan and turned back to Kara. "Here's my card," he said, removing a business card from his wallet. "Feel free to call me if you need anything."

"I will. Thank you."

When Kara looked up, he had disappeared into the crowded concourse.

Upon clearing customs, Kara engaged a redcap to help her with her luggage. Taking charge, the redcap snapped, "Follow me," and he proceeded to press his way through the throng of travelers milling about. Kara, almost running to keep up with him, was relieved at the chance to catch her breath when they took the escalator three flights down to the ground floor. The redcap collected her luggage from the Delta carousel and led her to the

closest exit where taxis were lined up at the curb
awaiting fares. The redcap loaded her luggage into
the trunk of the first cab in line and held the passenger door open for her.

"Here ya go, Miss."

"Thank you," Kara handed him a five-dollar tip
as she climbed into the rear seat of the cab. The
stench of unwashed bodies, cigarette smoke and
stale liquor made her stomach lurch.

"Where to, lady?" the cabbie asked as he
engaged the meter on the dash.

Kara fished around in her purse for the card
containing the address of her new apartment.
Finding it, she handed it to the driver.

The cabbie looked at the address, nodded his
head, and handed the card back to Kara. Then,
looking back over his shoulder, he pulled out into
traffic.

The taxi ride to the Graystone Apartments
was in and of itself another adventure. The driver
darted from one lane to another in-and-out of
traffic and slammed on the brakes only when he
absolutely had to. Otherwise, he barreled through
yellow lights with barely room to spare, all the
while talking over his shoulder about the NY Yankees and what their chances were of winning the
World Series this year. White knuckled, Kara sat
tightly gripping her handbag. She was too frightened to engage in conversation and hoped by
not encouraging him the driver would pay more
attention to the traffic. Arriving at the Graystone,
Kara jerked the passenger door open and struggled out of the seat. Her legs were weak from the

frightening ride, so she leaned against the cab taking deep breaths.

The driver, oblivious to Kara's situation and still chatting incessantly, transported her luggage from the trunk to the bank of elevators. Finally able to walk, Kara followed. Her hands were still shaking as she paid the fare. The cabbie summoned the elevator and when the doors opened, he swiveled his NY Yankees baseball cap around and placed Kara's luggage into the elevator. Stepping back, he bowed to her, turned, and jogged back out to his cab. Kara watched him leave. *Wonder how much longer that maniac has to live.*

CHAPTER 2

No Guts, No Glory

SCREEEEECH! The jarring sound echoed off the high-rise buildings lining the boulevard as an angry driver jammed his foot on the brake. The tires scorched the pavement and burned rubber as he careened to a halt. Behind him, an instantaneous chain reaction of vehicles breaking to a stop was accompanied by angry shouts, curses and blaring horns. The angry driver thrust his head out the window and glared at the female pedestrian who had stepped out into the street.

"Hey, ya dumb bitch! Watch where you're going! What are ya tryin' to do, commit suicide?" He muttered something else and extended his middle finger before he sped off down the boulevard.

Kara jumped back and scurried to the curb, looking over her shoulder as she did so. She was still getting used to New York and mentally chided herself for not paying attention when she stupidly stepped off the curb into oncoming traffic. Watching the jammed vehicles begin to unravel and angry drivers assess the damage wrought in the havoc, Kara felt her heart pounding in her chest and her cheeks flush with embarrassment.

She pulled her jacket closer across her chest and ducked her head in an attempt to remain as obscure as possible. She hurried along hoping to remain incognito as she became absorbed in the throng on the busy street.

Kara's high heels clicked rhythmically against the concrete as she hurried towards her destination. She glanced at her watch and quickened her pace. She stopped to get her bearings and, forgetting for the moment the ill-advised jaywalk, looked across at the sprawling United Nations plaza. In front of her, the colorful line of international flags stretched all the way from 42nd to 48th Street. Her destination was the Secretariat Building just beyond the long, low sweep of the Dag Hammarskjold Library, which was an odd contrast to the splendor of the glass UN high-rise.

Passing the visitors plaza, she stopped for a moment to look at a massive iron sculpture of a 45-caliber revolver with its barrel tied into a knot signifying non-violence. The artistic rendition with a mission had been presented to the UN by Luxembourg in 1988. Also on display was the Transatlantic Slave Trade Exhibition. Kara hurried past the exhibitions and shivered as she thought of her own roots, which were entrenched in both violence and slave trade. She entered the Secretariat Building through a set of heavy glass doors opening into a large lobby with high ceilings and polished stone floors.

Once inside, Kara joined the line waiting to pass through security. Several people in front set off the alarm and were sent back. Kara glanced at her watch; she was already late. Now it was her turn. Placing her purse, valise and jewelry on the conveyer belt, she stepped forward. The alarm sounded.

"Go back!" a security guard ordered in a gruff voice. "Put your shoes on the belt and try again."

Kara, incensed by the guard's attitude, did as she was told. She resented having to walk in her stocking feet across the platform that so many others had just passed through with dirty shoes. Finally clearing, she gathered up her belongings and took a few steps forward, hopping from foot to foot as she slipped on her shoes. She turned to her right and noticed a large INFORMATION sign translated into a dozen languages positioned above a curved wooden counter. It reminded her of a hotel check-in. Kara approached the desk and a stern looking woman looked up from the magazine she was perusing. She peered at Kara over her wire-rimmed glasses and brushed a stubborn strand of dull blonde hair back from her face. "May I help you?"

Already in a foul mood, Kara gingerly set her valise down and, frowning, rummaged through her shoulder bag. She handed the dour woman a sheaf of papers. The woman adjusted her glasses and scanned the documents. Without looking up, she picked up the phone and stabbed a series of numbers on the keypad. After a brief conversation, she replaced the receiver and fumbled around in a drawer until she came up with a pass card. She returned the papers to Kara along with the coded pass card and pointed her to a bank of elevators at the opposite end of the lobby. Kara hung the proffered lanyard with attached ID card around her neck and, jamming the paperwork back into her purse, hurried towards the elevators. *Oh, please God don't let the rest of the building's employees be as rude and unfriendly as security and that bitch.*

Two armed security officers turned and sized up Kara as she approached. The heavier of the two shifted from foot to foot. Kara lifted her pass card, and he glanced at it. Shifting again, he spoke into his shoulder mic and gestured toward the last elevator. The second guard accompanied her and passed his keycard through a slot adjacent to the elevator. "Your ID pass should be activated and will open the elevator doors," the officer told her. He held the door with his left hand, reached inside, and punched a button with his right. "Eleventh floor," he said and stepped back to allow Kara entry. "Spanish Embassy will be to your left."

"Thank you for your help," Kara replied as the door slid shut with a faint ding. The elevator whirled upward. Kara stepped from the elevator and entered through double wooden doors into a lushly appointed suite of offices. She approached the receptionist, identified as Miranda Lucero by the nameplate on her desk. "Hello, I'm Kara Isabella."

"Oh, yes, we've been expecting you." Miranda looked up, replacing the phone in its cradle. Kara surmised it had been a personal call judging from her giggly responses. Miranda hit the buzzer on the intercom. "I'll let Ambassador Madrid know you're here."

As she waited, Kara turned and surveyed the large reception area. It was tastefully appointed mixing various shades of mauve and blue. A plush blue carpet was a perfect canvas for the expensive array of mauve and blue sofas and chairs that were expertly arranged and accented with walnut glass-top coffee and end tables. Although one wall was glass from floor to ceiling overlooking 44th Street, table lamps were strategically positioned to soften the glare from the windows and provide a warm friendly atmosphere. Pictures of familiar landscapes native to Spain hung on the walls along with an array of plaques displaying various honors bestowed upon the Spanish Embassy.

The double doors at the far end of the room swung open, and a handsome Spaniard walked toward Kara.

"Kara!" Ambassador Madrid said, extending his hands. "I'm delighted to have you join our little family."

"Thank you, Ambassador. I'm happy to finally meet you."

"I've heard many good things about your language skills. I'm anxious to put them to the test. Lorraine has been gone for two weeks, and although I've managed—very awkwardly, I might add—to fend for myself, I'm feeling like an orphan. I'm certain you will enjoy working with the Spanish Embassy."

"I'm looking forward to working here. It's been a dream of mine for as long as I can remember."

"Come," Ambassador Madrid said as he took Kara by the arm. He led her through the suite of offices and introduced her to his staff along the way. Reaching the front of his office, he introduced her to Marti Ramos. Marti was assigned as Kara's assistant.

"Marti is one of our best," Ambassador Madrid assured her and nodded toward Marti, a small pretty woman in her late forties. She had flawless olive skin and Mediterranean features with brown eyes that were bright and intelligent. "She's been with the embassy for over five years and knows the building and its occupants as well as the security guards—a talent, which by the way, comes in handy from time-to-time. Marti's secretarial skills are unequaled, and she can transcribe from Spanish to English and vice-versa like no other. Since I'll be turning much of the transcribing and record keeping of our meetings over to you, you'll find Marti worth her weight in gold."

Kara extended her hand to her new assistant, "I am so pleased to meet you, Marti."

"And I you," Marti responded taking Kara's hand briefly. "I will continue the tour and show you to your office since the ambassador is running behind schedule this morning."

"Thank you, Marti," Ambassador Madrid said. He turned and, walking abruptly toward his office, added. "Take good care of our new addition." He stopped before closing his office door and, sticking his head out, said to Kara, "I'll come by later to update you on your assignments for the rest of the month and coordinate our calendars. Your hours are flexible since we have so many evening social functions to attend, but I'll want you here for all meetings."

"Pretty stingy with his time," Kara wanted to say but instead just bit her bottom lip.

"This way to your office, ma'am," Marti made a forward gesture. "Although it looks like it's a long way from the ambassador's office, it is actually directly behind his and you two have connecting doors, so you will be handy for translating on a moment's notice."

Marti handed Kara a new smart phone. "This will be your lifeline to communicate with the ambassador so keep it with you at all times. There is a tablet in your desk drawer."

Marti opened the door to Kara's office and stood aside so she could enter. Kara was pleasantly surprised by at its size and beauty. One wall was entirely windows draped with gossamer curtains, which diffused the morning sun. The furnishings mirrored those in the reception area. Kara circled around to the back of her impressive mahogany desk and sat down in the leather chair. She slowly swiveled sideways, taking in the entire panorama of her office and smiled with approval. It was all she had hoped for and more.

"I'll leave you so you can become acquainted with your new surroundings." Marti bent over the desk and wrote on a Post-it note. "This is your temporary password for computer access. Of course, you will want to change it. In case you're wondering, Rizado is the name of my mother's pet poodle. My extension is 817 and it's exclusively yours. It will never be busy when you call." Pointing to a pictured badge sitting on the desk, Marti said, "Your keycard. It has the photograph you submitted with your new hire paperwork. Guard it with your life. The badge you received when you arrived has limited access. This one allows you access to the building and every office in our suite except the ambassador's, of course." Then looking around, Marti asked, "Do you need anything?"

"No thank you, Marti. Oh, there is one thing. Please call me Kara. Ma'am is much too formal and Ms. Isabella is my mother's name. Other than that, I think I'm set."

"Yes ma'a....er, I mean Kara. That'll take some getting used to, but I'll manage. I'll bring you some fresh coffee and Danish if you like."

"I'll skip the Danish, but coffee sounds inviting—cream and sugar, two lumps please." Marti left and closed the door behind her. As she peered through the curtains at the skyline beyond, Kara's first impression of New York would be a lasting one. This was a dream job in a dream city, and so far, a dream come true.

CHAPTER 3

NOTHING VENTURED, NOTHING GAINED

MARK LANGFORD WAS WELL-KNOWN in Washington and other political circles. He was currently vying for his party's nomination to run for President and felt he had the inside track. However, his funds were rapidly dwindling and he needed a transfusion very badly.

Mark was genuinely attracted to Kara, so over the weekend, he took her advice and researched her ancestry online. He learned she was the only child and heir of Giovanni Isabella, one of the wealthiest men in the world. *Manna from heaven.* Mark's interest in Kara spiked as he recognized the value of being aligned with the Isabellas.

The following Monday, Mark made it a point to visit the Spanish Embassy. He telephoned and set up an appointment to see the ambassador after lunch to give credence to his unscheduled visit. He was really there to see Kara.

Upon his arrival, Mark told Miranda to let Kara know he was there to see her. Miranda dialed Kara's extension, "Senator Langford is here to see you."

"He's here?"

"Standing right here," Miranda winked at Mark, who was leaning on her counter.

"Okay . . . ah . . . what does he want?

"He didn't say, just asked to see you."

"Let me have that," Mark took the phone from Miranda's hand. But before he could speak, he heard Kara say, "Okay, send him back."

Handing the phone back to Miranda, Mark adjusted his suit jacket, pinched Miranda's cheek, and walked toward Kara's office.

He knocked first and stuck his head in. He found her absorbed in paperwork.

"See you made it through customs," he joked.

"Customs was a breeze. The taxi ride was suicide."

"You can tell me all about it over lunch. Will you join me?"

"Thank you, I would like that. The ambassador is spending the afternoon at home. He's hosting a small dinner party this evening so I'm free for a couple of hours." Mark noticed Kara was barefoot when she stood and retrieved her jacket from the back of her chair.

"I know. Ambassador Madrid has ordered my appearance. Perhaps I could pick you up . . ." Mark said as he held her office door open and waited for her to slip into her shoes and adjust her jacket.

"There, I'm ready," she smiled and pointed to her feet. "New shoes."

"Know the feeling. The restaurant is only a couple of blocks from here, but we could drive if you'd rather?"

"I'm fine. My feet just needed to be pampered."

Mark held his arm out and she accepted the offer by sliding her arm into his.

Leaving the embassy, the couple walked the few short blocks to *The Forum*, an old established restaurant so named because the décor mirrored that of the senate floor. After being seated, a waiter handed Mark and Kara menus and retreated.

Kara perused the menu. The names of the entrees intrigued her, and she laughed as she read aloud. "Caesar Salad, Orange Judas, Nero Sandwich, Et tu Brute Kabob! Now, that's cruel."

"Yes, the owners are clever and quite merciless," Mark replied, looking at his menu. "The special, Grilled Salmon Filibuster, looks good."

Kara put her menu aside, "How long have you been with the Spanish delegation, Mark?" she queried.

"H-m-m-m, actually, let's see, I was appointed a year ago when Spain was on the verge of collapse due to the country's failing economy. My function is to assist in economic restructure. I report directly to Vice President Bartholomew Morris."

"Sounds technical. What kind of education does one need to restructure a country's economy?"

The waiter reappeared and Mark looked at Kara. "Have you decided?"

"I'll have the Speaker's Chef Salad with the House Dressing on the side."

"Very good, Madam. And you, Sir?"

"Think I'll try the salmon special."

"What would you like to drink?" the waiter asked as he accepted Kara's menu.

"I just can't resist the Iced Mark Anthon-tea," Kara said.

The waiter smiled and arched his eyebrows as he looked at Mark.

"I'll have the same." He handed his menu to the waiter and turned his attention back to Kara. "I earned my JD from Indiana University and also hold dual masters in Socioeconomics and Political Science, as well as in International Business Law and Globalization from Utrecht University in Utrecht, Netherlands. I guess the powers that be decided I was qualified enough and here I am."

"I'm impressed with your credentials, and I'm sure your constituents are as well."

"Why, thank you. But we've been talking a lot about me, Kara. Now, tell me about you."

"Where to start? As you probably know by now, provided you did your homework assignment, I'm the only child of Giovanni and Louisa Isabella and literally grew up in a castle in Spain . . . as they say in the song."

Mark smiled. "I'm familiar with that song; my sister played *Castles in Spain* in a violin recital."

"Does she live here?"

"No, Vonnie married right out of high school. She lives in Kokomo with her husband and three children."

"Kokomo?"

"Kokomo, Indiana, that is. Not the exotic tropical island. You were saying. . . ."

"Upon graduation from high school, I went to Complutense University in Madrid, majoring in language and eventually receiving a proficiency certification in English, French, Portuguese, Galician and Arabic."

Mark raised his eyebrows in admiration.

"Several months after graduating from the university, I became restless and bored. My friends were scattered, either attending a distant university or in some cases, married and starting families of their own. I wanted to use my education, but teaching didn't appeal to me. I don't have the patience to cope with teens." Kara took a sip of tea and gently flipped her hair back over her shoulder.

"What brought you to the States?"

"One lazy afternoon leafing through a magazine, I saw an article on the United Nations and was mesmerized with the layout depicting the UN and the skyline of New York City. At that moment, I decided that was it. That's what I wanted to do with my language skills—be an interpreter at the UN and live in New York City.

"I found Daddy in the courtyard and told him. After the initial shock, he was very supportive. Businessman that he is, he apparently saw the benefit in my making worldwide connections. Mother, on the other hand, was not as enamored and expressed worry about me being on my own in New York City 'of all places.' They had a pretty heated discussion and in the end, Daddy told Mother, 'Enough! My mind is set. I will see that Kara gets the appointment.' Mother said something like, 'Of course you will. Why did you even ask me?' and Daddy responded, 'I didn't ask you, I told you. There's a difference.'" Kara punctuated the scene by defiantly folding her arms across her chest when she mimicked Daddy and waving them wildly around when she imitated Mother.

She finished with a sweep of her hand and looked determinedly at Mark, "So, you see, here I am."

"Defiant creature," Mark commented.

"Determined would be a better term. Once I set my mind on something, I find a way to make it happen. I usually get what I pray for!"

"I guess you have to be careful what you pray for."

Kara watched Mark's face turn crimson. It was then he revealed his boyish side, and Kara concluded that he could be manipulated every bit as easy as her father. At least, so she thought.

"Tell me, what was it like growing up in a castle?"

"You're certainly making a big deal over an ordinary every day run-of-the-mill castle," Kara teased.

"I guess it's . . . intriguing. I don't know many castle-dwellers. How is it your family took up residence in a castle in the first place?"

"Good question, Mark! Five hundred or so years ago life was expendable. My ancestors were involved in some unsavory practices and needed a fortress for protection."

Mark flinched. "What kind of unsavory practices?"

"Mostly slave trade but they also engaged in pirating, pillaging and plundering. You know the old saying, to the victor goes the spoils. All in all, their exploits amassed the family a fortune. The family motto, *Intimidate and Conquer*, is something my forefathers did on a grand scale, and truth be known, still do."

Mark flinched again, "Still do?"

"Still do, but not so violently."

Kara watched Mark fidget with his water glass. *I hope he isn't thinking Mafia.* "However, today's endeavors are political, not physical," she added.

"Oh, I see." The relief in Mark's voice was perceptible.

"The controlling families eventually lost their lust for blood, the age-old hostilities burned out, and the countryside finally calmed down. Although the estate is now peaceful and dreamy, it wasn't always that way.

"As a child, it was easy to pretend to be a princess within the walls of the ancient but stately *Castillo de Isabella*, the jewel of the countryside. The family home was modeled after the prominent Spanish castle, *Castillo de Coca*, but on a much smaller scale. *De Coca* is the epitome of castles. Look it up on the net. You should take the tour the next time you visit Spain. It's well worth the effort."

"I'm beyond fascinated. Perhaps you could accompany me and be my tour guide."

"Whoa, I just got here. I'm not ready to go rounds with Mother anytime soon. How often are you required to visit my homeland?"

"Depends, usually every three months."

"Well, maybe by then . . . My goodness. I don't usually talk this much and especially about myself. Am I boring you?"

"Boring me! Absolutely not!" Mark took a drink of tea, rested his elbow on the table, and leaned toward Kara. "Tell me more. I want to know everything about you. It's fascinating. Please continue."

"As a child, I didn't have many playmates. We lived too far from civilization. Daddy taught me to ride; I became an accomplished equestrian at a very young age and spent a lot of time riding Rocinante.

"Rocinante? Don Quixote's horse was named Rocinante."

"You must be well read. Not many people recognize that. I admire people who are versed in literature. Roc was originally Santa Maria, but I renamed him after Mother read me the story of Don Quixote. Daddy has a stable of Lipizzans; three of his show horses are named Niña, Pinta and Santa Maria. When Daddy gave me Santa Maria, I renamed him."

"How'd that go over with your father?"

"He did say, 'It's your horse and you can call him anything you like.' However, Daddy mentioned Columbus would probably run him through for letting me get away with insulting his fleet. I told Daddy I didn't want people to think I had named my horse after an ancient ship or an active volcano in Guatemala. He then reached into his pocket and pulled out a white handkerchief and waived it in mock surrender."

Mark doubled over with laughter. Kara had captivated him. *She's unlike anyone I've ever known*

and she has a lot of spunk. I like that. I can't remem-
ber having this much fun with a woman outside the
sheets ever! She's beautiful, intelligent, entertain-
ing and apparently has her wealthy father wrapped
around her little finger. What more could a politician
want?

"Are you all right? You're having so much fun
that I'm beginning to think maybe I should also
have ordered the Filibuster special."

"I'm fine. In fact, I'm having the time of my life.
Please. . . ."

"Try to control yourself, people are staring."

"Good. I need the notoriety."

"Being dubbed an imbecile could not possibly
enhance your political career."

"You sure? From what I've seen in DC, that's
a plus . . . ."

"Shhhh." Kara put her finger to her lips. "To
continue, well-rounded castle-dwellers play piano
according to Mother. She tried to teach me; she
plays like an angel. I'd never be able to match her
skill but I tried. I do all right, that is as long as it's
chopsticks."

"You'll have to play for me sometime," Mark
said as he fidgeted with the lemon wedge in his
tea glass.

"Unlike most wealthy children, I spent a lot
of time in the kitchen. I loved watching our chef,
Lorenzo, create culinary delights. He taught me
how to cook. Some evening after I get settled, I'll
fix you a dinner you won't soon forget."

"I'll hold you to that promise." Then, looking at
his watch, Mark said, "My God, Kara, look at the

time, the afternoon has flown by. I could listen to you all day, but the taxpayers deserve better of me, and although I hate to say it, we need to get back on the time clock."

Kara glanced at her watch. "You're right. We should go."

Mark held her chair as they rose to leave, saying, "*The Forum* is a gathering place for a lot of the embassy's employees. I've made valuable contacts here. When we have more time, I'll introduce you around."

Returning to the Spanish Embassy, Mark expressed his desire to pick Kara up and accompany her to the ambassador's dinner party.

"Yes, I would like that. Since I don't know my way around, being chauffeured would ease the stress. And thank you for such a delightful lunch"

"It is I who should be thanking you. Did you see the looks of envy from my colleagues? I'll pick you up at six. I think the ambassador is back and I need to see him before tonight." As he turned to leave, Mark managed to give Kara a quick kiss on the cheek before disappearing down the corridor. Little did they know, but the kiss on the cheek would become a tradition between the two of them throughout their relationship.

After leaving Kara at her office, Mark could concentrate only on his anticipated evening with her. He wanted it to be a memorable occasion. He called his secretary and requested she make arrangements for a horse-drawn carriage to be available when he returned Kara to her apartment that evening. He hoped that would set the tone for the remainder of the evening.

After a brief meeting with the ambassador, Mark swung by his campaign headquarters located on Mulberry Street in the heart of NYC. Just as he was entering the offices, he encountered his campaign manager, Fletcher Russell, who was leaving.

"Hey, Mark!"

"Fletch, glad I caught you."

"I'm surprised to see you. Thought you'd be indisposed the rest of the afternoon," Fletcher said, slapping Mark on the back.

"Why?"

"I had lunch with some of the guys at *The Forum* and couldn't help notice you, you lucky bastard, lunching with the most lovely creature I've ever seen. It looked like the two of you were thoroughly enjoying each other's company. The thought occurred to me that the two of you might be indulging in dessert at a more private venue. Who is she anyway?"

"This *is* my lucky day. . . but not *that* lucky. That lovely creature is Kara Isabella. Have you heard of Giovanni Isabella, one of the richest men in the world?"

"She's the daughter of *that* Isabella?"

"One and the same."

"Why, you sly old dog," Fletch said in a seductive voice. "Do you always come up smelling like a rose?"

"Yeah, right! How long have you known me?"

"Point well taken," Fletch teased.

"But. . .as it turns out, Kara decided she wanted to expand her horizons beyond the confines of her castle in Spain. Can't say I blame her. That must have been a tough decision."

"Sure, sure. Don't throw me in that briar patch. . . ."

"You're safe, Fletch. Only Prince Charmings are relegated to castles. Anyway, to continue the saga, *Daddy* arranged for her to replace Lorraine as an interpreter at the Spanish Embassy. I actually met Kara on the plane returning from my last trip. We were seatmates. H-m-m-m, maybe I should buy some lottery tickets."

"Judging from the way the two of you were carrying on, you won't need them. Do you think Daddy could be persuaded to contribute to the cause?"

"I intend to work on that."

"I'll just bet you do. Better get a move on. We're running out of time."

"You don't have to remind me. Twenty-three months, seven days and," looking at his watch, Mark continued, "fourteen hours and twenty-seven minutes."

"And here I thought you didn't know the time of day," Fletch joshed.

"I'm keeping my eye on the ball, Fletch. You just do your job and I'll do mine."

"Roger that. I'm on my way over to the TV station to view our latest commercial. Keep me posted on the exploits of Beauty and the Beast."

"Very funny. But . . . don't you be calling Kara a beast."

The two men shared a hardy laugh as they parted and went their separate ways.

"Mark, Kara, come in, come in!" Ambassador Madrid exclaimed. The ambassador and his wife, Alejandra, stood in the foyer greeting guests as they were ushered in.

"Good evening, Ambassador." Mark shook Madrid's hand. "And, Alejandra, you look lovely as always. Thank you for inviting me."

"Why, Mark, we always look forward to your presence at our gatherings. It just wouldn't be the same without you. And, Kara, I'm finally pleased to meet you," Alejandra said.

"Thank you, and I you," Kara said taking Alejandra's hand.

"The ambassador tells me he doesn't know how he got along without you."

"I understand he did pretty well the two weeks he was on his own. But, being indispensable works for me, let's let him keep thinking that," Kara joked.

"You're learning," Alejandra said. "You're the last to arrive. Let's join the others. I could use a toddy before we dine; how about you?"

"Yes, thank you," Kara answered as they entered the living room with the ambassador and Mark close behind.

"What would you like to drink?" Alejandra asked Kara and Mark as she motioned to the butler.

"A glass of white wine would be just fine," Kara responded.

"Make that two," Mark said.

The butler acknowledged with a nod of his head. "Very well, sir."

"Make that three. The ambassador already has his drink," Alejandra said and the butler retreated to the bar.

"Do you know everyone here?" Mark whispered to Kara as he looked around the room.

Looking at the six other guests, Kara nodded. "I believe I've met everyone through the embassy."

Just then, the butler reappeared with the wine and, leaning toward Alejandra, quietly spoke to her.

"Thank you, Richard." Then Alejandra said loud enough for all to hear, "Dinner is ready. Ambassador, if you please."

Ambassador Madrid set his glass on the bar and beckoned all to follow as he took Alejandra's arm and led the small dinner party to the opulent dining room.

Dinner was delectable and the party was lively. Everyone appeared to be enjoying the evening. After dessert, the hosts ushered their guests into the drawing room. Mark, noticing fatigue on the ambassador's face, said to Kara, "I think we should leave soon. Our host is fading."

Kara nodded and the two of them stood, signaling their departure. The other guests took the hint and followed their lead.

"Good night, thank you for coming," the host and hostess said to each guest as they departed.

Kara responded. "I thoroughly enjoyed the evening."

"And we enjoyed having you. I look forward to seeing you again soon," Alejandra said.

Once outside, Mark took Kara's wrap and gently put it around her shoulders "Hope you're not in a hurry to get home," he said. "It's still early— well, by New York standards anyway. I want to show you *my* New York. Are you up to a mini tour of the city?"

"Absolutely! I haven't done much sightseeing. The only landmark I've seen is the Statue of Liberty, and that was from the air. You were with me then."

"Well then, what are we waiting for?" he said, holding the passenger door of his black Cadillac XTS open for Kara. "Fasten your seatbelt and hang on. Here we go." Mark made the tour sound like a carnival ride much to Kara's delight.

Mark headed for the heart of the city. The boulevards were awash with lights and, judging from the throngs parading up and down the avenues, it appeared New Yorkers never slept. Mark watched Kara as she swiveled her head in all directions trying to take in the sights.

"This is hypnotizing, Mark. It looks like a movie set. Is Times Square always this crowded?"

"I don't know about always, but when I've been here, it is."

They passed famous landmarks: the new World Trade Center, Rockefeller Center, Brooklyn

Bridge and Radio City Music Hall. He told her Radio City was nicknamed the "Showplace of the Nation." Kara peered into the windows as they slowly drove by. Observing her special interest, Mark said, "Radio City is the home of the famous and fabulous Rockettes. Someday I'll take you to one of their performances."

"I'll hold you to that," Kara replied and the deal was sealed with a handshake.

Mark concluded the tour in Kara's neighborhood, "I have a surprise for you." He parked in a lot close to where a horse drawn buggy awaited them.

Taking her hand, Mark exclaimed, "Come on, Princess. Your carriage awaits."

Kara looked at Mark with wide eyes as he tugged her by the hand toward the buggy. She giggled when he boosted her up onto the red velvet carriage seat. He gracefully slid into the seat beside her and put his arm around her shoulders, "Just in case you get cold," he whispered in her ear.

The carriage was white with gold trim and Rolland, the driver, was dressed in a red waistcoat atop black trousers. Looking back to determine if the couple was secure, Rolland looked to Mark for approval to proceed. Mark had grown up in Indianapolis, so it was inevitable he would say, "Gentlemen, start your engines," as he pointed at the docile source of power standing by patiently waiting. Rolland laughed and tipped his hat in appreciation of Mark's humor.

"That's the first time Dancer has been referred to as a gentleman," Rolland said. He gave the gray a stinging nudge with the buggy whip, whistled and shouted, "Come on, Dancer, let's go girl." The gray looked back over her shoulder, whinnied, and pranced out in grand style as Rolland said loud enough for Kara and Mark to hear, "See why I call 'er Dancer?" The clippity-clop of Dancer's hoofs against the asphalt was relaxing, and the couple cuddled in the comfort of the plush carriage seat as they jostled along through Central Park in the cool of the evening.

"I've heard Central Park isn't safe after dark," Kara said as Mark pulled her close.

"Have no fear, my pretty, you're with the brave Senator from Indiana, and no one would dare challenge him. Besides, Rolland is armed and is an ex-marine."

Kara playfully punched him on the upper arm and couldn't help notice the firmness and size of his bicep. The excursion was invigorating and the park was inviting despite the nasty reputation of villains lurking in the shadows. The gray reminded Kara of Rocinante, and she was surprised at a sudden twinge of homesickness. However, she couldn't remain melancholy for long in Mark's company. He was knowledgeable and witty and kept up a constant flow of rhetoric both informative and entertaining.

After exactly one hour, Rolland directed Dancer back to the exact spot where they had started. He jumped down from the driver's seat, patted Dancer on the rump, and walking around to the front of the horse, offered her an apple, which she daintily took between her bared teeth and placed on the pavement. She whinnied once before attacking the apple and crunching it. "That's Dancer's way of thankin' me," Rolland said to Mark, who had just alighted from the carriage. Mark laughed as he helped Kara to the pavement.

"And you, my friend, made this evening one to remember. Thank you for the exceptional service," Mark said as he handed Rolland a fifty-dollar bill.

Rolland snapped his hand to his hat in salute, "Thank you, Governor. The pleasure was all mine." He smiled and nodded to Kara before climbing back onto the driver's seat and directing Dancer in the direction of Central Park.

The cool nocturnal air was alluring, and the noisy hum of the city traffic was left behind as Mark and Kara walked arm-in-arm in the direction of Kara's apartment a block away. Kara rummaged around in her purse searching for her door key. Finally finding it, she opened the door and looked into Mark's eyes, "Thank you, Senator, for a lovely evening. I hope you don't mind if I don't invite you in. I'm still getting acclimated and am fatigued by the end of day."

"I totally understand. When I travel, I experience jet lag and all that goes with it, so I know how you're feeling. May I call you again?"

"Of course. I would be delighted. I'll surely see you at the embassy. Perhaps by that time, I will have overcome this malady."

Kara noticed Mark's disappointment at the sudden end to an enchanting evening. However, he did manage to kiss Kara gently on the cheek before she stepped inside her apartment. Kara softly closed her door and leaned against the jamb. *I could become interested in the handsome Senator from Indiana.*

CHAPTER 4

WHAT YOU DON'T KNOW
WON'T HURT YOU

ALTHOUGH MARK WAS MESMERIZED by Kara's beauty and charm, he was more interested in her father's vast wealth and powerful connections. Several months into their relationship, Mark proposed to Kara. He had done his research well, and the cunning individual that he was, he determined fairly early on that Giovanni would ensure that his daughter became First Lady.

With that goal in mind and, because the election was only eighteen months away, Mark ratcheted up his pursuit and embarked on a whirlwind courtship. He took Kara places and showed her sights she had never heard of, much less seen. When they went on the buggy ride with Rolland and Dancer a few months earlier, they toured the traditional attractions. Since that time, Mark had been showing her the sights not so well publicized but very popular with the locals. Each weekend they engaged in a new adventure.

"Hello, handsome," Kara answered.

"Hello yourself, gorgeous. I'm on the turnpike just approaching the city. Will be there soon. I have something very special planned for us. Can you be ready in an hour?"

Mark loved Kara's spontaneity and smiled when she squealed in his ear. "You betcha! Give me a clue so I'll know what to wear."

"H-m-m-m, the only clue you get is dress casual."

"That's not fair. You're probably wearing my favorite navy blue suit."

"Not so, I'm so casual you may not want to be seen with me."

"That'll be the day."

"Oops, gotta pay attention to my driving, getting into some heavy traffic—see you soon."

"Can hardly wait."

For the afternoon, Mark had planned an excursion that included a visit to the Jefferson Market Courthouse. Erected in the late 1800s, the structure was adorned with turrets, gables, stained-glass windows and a fantastic clock tower. After visiting the courthouse, he would take her to Bleecker and Commerce Streets to do some shopping, followed by lunch at the Spotted Pig, a very popular restaurant some called the Gastropub.

Not wanting to take the chance of losing Kara and, of course, her father's wealth and influence, Mark planned this day to propose. *I want this to be a special and memorable day to impress Daddy, so I'll wind up the afternoon at Tiffany's and let her pick out an engagement ring. A small cost compared to the large return. I can only hope she takes it well when I explain to her she'll have to wait to wear it or even tell anyone about our commitment since she's not a U.S. citizen. Having a foreigner as First Lady might not set well with my constituents. What she doesn't need to know is that I don't want to disillusion the female voters. If I'm perceived as being out of circulation, they may not vote for me.*

Mark had called *Tiffany's* and set an appointment for late afternoon and requested a private showing. The jeweler was very accommodating.

Mark parked in a no parking zone in front of the Graystone, a perk that came with his Senator status. Kara opened her apartment door, and Mark took a quick breath. Even in jeans and a T-shirt, she looked stunning.

"This casual enough?" Kara then swirled like a figure skater.

"Honey, you'd look like a million bucks in a paper sack."

"With an approval rating like that, I can't miss. And you don't look too bad yourself."

Not taking time to enter her apartment, Mark grabbed her by the hand and pulled her out into the corridor. Holding her tightly, he kissed her passionately. Kara succumbed as she pulled the door shut behind her.

"If this is a prelude to your surprise weekend, I'm all in," she said.

"Call it an appetizer. I just couldn't control myself when I saw you standing there," Mark said as they walked to the elevators.

Mark had planned well and the day was spent sightseeing, shopping, and sampling a variety of eats from many vendors they encountered. After they gorged themselves at the Spotted Pig, Mark said, "I need to run into Manhattan for a few minutes. Are you up to one more stop?"

"Absolutely! What are you doing in Manhattan?"

"It's business and pleasure," Mark responded as he pulled into the *Tiffany's* parking lot.

Mark jumped out of the car and ran around to open the passenger door, offering Kara his hand. *Maybe this is laying it on a little thick, but what the hell. . . .*

Kara smiled up at Mark as she took his hand. "I don't know what's going on but I like it."When they entered the jewelry store, Mark noticed even Kara, a worldwide shopper, was wide-eyed at the store's opulence. They were escorted to a private viewing room, which included champagne and caviar.

"Mark, what is this. . . ?"

"This, my darling, is my unique way of asking you to marry me. I wanted an occasion we could remember when we're old and gray, sitting on the veranda in our rocking chairs."

"Mark. . .this is. . .sudden. . .unexpected!"

"Not for me, I've waited a lifetime for you."

Looking at Mark through tear-filled eyes, Kara sat open-mouthed as the jewelry associates began bringing in trays of diamond rings.

"But I. . .I don't know what to say."

"For starters, you could tell me you love me."

"I. . .I'm not sure I can make a commitment."

"I'm sure enough for both of us. You better choose a ring, they close at seven." *Damn it, I thought she would jump at the chance to marry me and become First Lady.*

Kara took the glass of champagne proffered by an associate and emptied it in one gulp. She held her glass for a refill and, taking her time, began to ogle the trays of diamond rings. Mark sat silently and watched as Kara examined ring after ring. She reminded him of a kid in a candy store. After about twenty minutes, Kara stood with a broad smile and held up one of the largest diamonds on the tray. She looked at Mark and said, "This one, I want this one. And look, it fits. It was meant to be."

Mark motioned for an associate to process the purchase. He knew the price would be beyond his means but it didn't matter. Whatever she wanted, he was willing to give her. A few minutes later the associate reappeared with the signature *Tiffany's* turquoise ring box containing the purchase and an invoice. Kara took the box and extracted the ring. Holding it up, she said, "Look how it twinkles."

Mark's first impression was that it looked like a searchlight at a movie premier. He took the invoice and didn't even glance at it for fear the look on his face would reveal what he was really thinking. Instead, he simply placed his credit card on the tray and handed it to the associate with an air of nonchalance.

"Thank you, sir. I'll be right back."

Mark noticed Kara studying the ring. Then she said, "Mark, this is all very nice, but. . . ."

Oh, my God. I buy her a fifty thousand dollar engagement ring, and there's a but attached? "But what?" he asked, stifling as much irritation from his voice as possible.

"But you haven't said the words."

"What? Oh, the words. How insensitive of me." Mark went down on one knee, took Kara's hand and, taking the ring, slipped the ring on her finger, saying, "Kara, will you marry me?"

"H-m-m-m-m, that's not very romantic."

If this is a preview of what life is going to be like with her, maybe I should just ride off into the sunset—alone. "Okay, let's try that again. Kara, my darling, I love you with all my heart and want to spend the rest of my life with you. Will you marry me?" He hoped his proposal sounded more sincere than he felt at the moment.

"Guess that'll have to do," Kara groused. "And, yes, I will marry you."

Wonder how she's going to react when I tell her we have to keep our engagement under wraps. Sure can't do that now or anytime soon. A voice inside whispered, *Sooner than later!*

The associate returned and handed Mark the credit card receipt. Mark scribbled his name across the bottom and jammed his copy into his pocket.

"Let's go so we can beat the rush-hour traffic," he said to Kara. Her reaction and complacency were gnawing at him.

Mark pondered the approach he would take in requesting that she keep their engagement secret. When they arrived at Kara's apartment, he blurted, "I have a request to make and hope you won't take it the wrong way."

Kara flinched. "You're not asking that I return the ring, are you?"

"No, of course not. But, you know I'm favored to be my party's presidential nominee. . ."

"Yes, I know that."

"You also know how fickle voters are."

"Where is this going, Mark?"

"What I'm asking, darling, is that you to keep our engagement under wraps until after the election."

Kara squinted. "But why?" she asked.

"My major concern is that the electorate will frown upon a foreigner becoming First Lady. I hope you understand. I do want to marry you but. . .I also want to be President of the United States. I guess you might say I want my cake and eat it, too."

"Mark, I was worried for a moment you had changed your mind."

"I knew you'd understand."

"Of course. Speaking of which, you haven't said much about the campaign. Is it going well?"

"Uh, oh, fair. Of course, it's too early to make any predictions but. . ."

"But what? Is there anything I can do to help you?"

"I don't want to burden you with my problems," Mark replied.

"As of this afternoon, they're not just your problems."

"Since you put it that way, donations are down and my funds are dwindling. In fact, my war chest is almost empty. It takes money to generate votes."

"Money! Is that all? Why didn't you tell me sooner? Daddy will know what to do. Not only will he contribute but his cronies will as well. All I have to do is ask."

"How can you be so sure?"

"You don't know Daddy. As soon as I tell him about our engagement, he'll be eager to assist in any way he can. He has backed a number of successful candidates here and abroad. With Daddy's help you can concentrate on more important aspects of the campaign."

"Can I take that to the bank?"

"In more ways than one."

"Must be my lucky day."

"Mine, too!"

As soon as Mark left, Kara called her father.

"Daddy! You'll never guess what!" she said excitedly.

"You're coming home on vacation?"

"Better than that! Mark just proposed. Do you know what that means if Mark is elected President of the United States?"

"Of course. It means my daughter will be First Lady . . . ."

"Daddy, Mark is a dream come true. Even if he is not elected, I'll love him just the same. Being married to the President of the United States is just the frosting on the cake."

"But. . . ."

"I know. This is sudden and a shock to say the least."

"I can't wait to pass on the news to your mother."

"Daddy, you can't tell Mother just yet."

"Can't tell you mother? Pray tell me, why not?"

"Mark has made me promise to keep our engagement a closely guarded secret until after the election. I agreed once I heard his reasoning. He fears that Americans would balk at having a foreigner as First Lady. After he's elected, we'll announce it. What could his constituents do about it then?"

"Kara, your mother should be the first to know, not the last. She will be very happy for you."

"But, Daddy, you know how Mother likes to brag. There's no way she could keep my engagement a secret. Haven't you always said, 'If you want to make something public, telephone, telegraph or tell Louisa'."

"It appears I'm caught in my own trap, so I give you my pledge of secrecy. But we can't keep your mother in the dark forever. How long before the election?"

"Eighteen months, Daddy. And when she finds out, she'll be so happy she won't sulk over not knowing sooner. In the interim, I have another request."

"I'm listening."

"Mark is running low on funding and with the election only eighteen months away, he should be gearing up his campaign but money is so tight. . . .Is there anyway. . . ."

"Say no more. Have him telephone me and I will make sure that he receives an adequate donation. I'll call in some markers on this end to ensure he is elected. I find this sort of thing. . . invigorating."

"Oh, Daddy, you're a dear! I knew you would help. Mark will forever be in your debt."

"That's exactly what I'm counting on. What's that old Yankee saying, *There's no such thing as a free lunch.*"

When he hung up, Kara's father swiveled his chair around, and from his second story office, took a deep breath and inhaled the scent of expanded power. Kara, in the meanwhile, could picture her father scheming as to how he would cash in on his contemplated campaign contribution.

Kara phoned Mark the next day.

"Langford," it was Sunday and Mark's office staff was off for the weekend, so he answered the phone.

"Hey, handsome, you dismiss all the help?"

"I've been relegated to doing double duty since it's Sunday. Not many calls on the weekend and ordinarily I don't answer the phone on weekends. But I thought it might be you. What a pleasant surprise."

"Well, you're in for another pleasant surprise. I talked to Daddy. He has pledged to help you financially and do what he can to ensure your election." Silence on the other end of the line. After what seemed to Kara like an eternity, she asked, "You still there?"

"Good thing I'm sitting down, my knees suddenly became weak. I'm speechless. . . ."

"That'd be a first. . ."

"You're not playing with me, are you?"

"Not now. Saving that for later."

"So, you're serious about what your father said."

"Absolutely!"

"My God!"

"Honey, believe me. If Daddy says he will do something, consider it done. He wants you to contact him and he will make arrangements to have a sizable sum transferred to you right away. Legally, of course. He knows how to finesse these things. In his experience, he opined, once the ball gets rolling, your supporters will find a way to keep the cash coming in. His telephone number is on the back of the card I gave you that has my telephone numbers on it, both here and in Spain."

"What's a sizable sum?"

"Daddy didn't give me a figure. That is something you need to discuss with him."

After a slight pause, Mark said, "I'd like to see you tonight."

"I'd like to see you, too."

"If you'll put me up for the night, I'll buy dinner."

"Promise?"

"Promise."

Since Kara couldn't wear her engagement ring, she put it inside a secret zippered compartment on the underside of a small stuffed scruffy lion where she knew it would be safe. Who would look for treasure inside a beat-up stuffed animal? The lion was a gift from her Aunt Sophie when Kara turned eight. As she zipped the hidden compartment, she relived the day in mid-August some twenty years before when Aunt Sophie came for a visit and brought the lion all the way from Paris. Kara could still picture how she and Aunt Sophie sat by the fountain in the courtyard at the castle as she enthusiastically tore the wrappings aside, extracting the stuffed toy from the packaging. It was no secret she liked stuffed animals and her Aunt Sophie was not known to disappoint. She remembered Aunt Sophie helping her name the new addition. Scruffy was the name they both agreed upon.

"Your lion has a secret. See if you can find it," Aunt Sophie had said.

Kara carefully examined Scruffy from top to bottom but didn't detect anything out of the ordinary.

"Here, let me help you." Sophie gently took Scruffy and showed Kara the hidden compartment. "Now, you unzip this to find the ideal hiding place for what's contained inside."

Kara remembered the delight she experienced when she found a charm bracelet smuggled inside the hidden compartment. She gave her aunt a heart-felt hug and together they examined the charms one-by-one. Sophie told her, "The horse charm is Rocinante; the crown is you, the princess of *Castillo de Isabella*; the lion, your astrological sign, is Scruffy; the heart is to remind you that I love you; and the star is the one you wish upon to make your dreams come true."

Kara remembered wearing the bracelet well into her teens until the clasp broke. Utilizing a paperclip, she repaired it and fastened it around Scruffy's neck where it had since remained.

Aunt Sophie studied stars and horoscopes and Kara was fascinated by her predictions. Thinking back to that day at the fountain, Kara could still hear Aunt Sophie's prediction, "Kara, my child, on this your eighth birthday, the stars tell me your future husband will be a very handsome, wealthy, influential man. He will sweep you off your feet and you will melt in his arms. You will live in a far-away land and find happiness beyond your wildest imagination." She remembered her aunt's eyes narrowed with warning. "Be wary and not in a hurry to marry."

As she held the lion, Kara wondered if Mark was the end or the means to the end. In any event, she would heed her aunt's admonition and be discerning.

The weekend passed much too quickly and Kara found herself totally unprepared for another harried week. A stack of unfinished work awaited her. Distracted by Mark's proposal and fantasizing about the future, she sorted through the paperwork until she noticed the time.

"Oh, my God, I'm late." She fumbled for a file, which resulted in her spilling her coffee. She piled handfuls of tissue on the spill and bolted out the door. Kara looked dejectedly at her watch as the elevator finally came to a stop on the first floor. She hurried from the building into the blinding sunlight and dodged heavy traffic, rushing to make it on time for her appointment at *BellaDonna's*. The frivolity of the appointment made her wonder if maybe she should reschedule. Looking at her nails, she knew otherwise. First things first. Her appearance or perceived appearance dictated how well she would perform. Self-confidence in her appearance translated into self-confidence in the performance of her assigned tasks. She would do well if she looked and felt good. Over the years, her mindset had changed little.

As Kara breathlessly pushed through the doors of the salon, a perky receptionist dressed in a Romanesque toga peered across the marble reception desk. The woman smiled and asked, "Do you have an appointment?"

"Yes, thank you, Anna." Kara said, looking at the nametag attached to the toga. "I had an appointment for three-thirty, and I apologize for being a little late. My name is Kara Isabella."

Looking at the appointment book, Anna said, "Of course, I have you scheduled with Gabrielle. She is one of our best manicurists. She's waiting for you. Please, come this way." She led Kara to Gabrielle's station, her Roman-style flip-flops snapping against her feet as she walked.

At Gabrielle's station, Anna announced, "This is Kara, your three-thirty appointment." She turned and flip-flopped her way back to the reception desk.

The manicurist shook Kara's hand and said, "I'm Gabrielle." She gestured for Kara to be seated.

"Thank you for waiting, I really appreciate it. I'm in a bind. Do you think you could do my nails in double time?"

"I'll try my best," Gabrielle replied as she began pulling bottles, nail files, and cotton balls from a drawer in her station. As she was stripping Kara's polish, Kara noticed a shadow pass across the workstation. She heard a female voice say, "Hey, I came back early. Vermont was lovely but boring. Aunt Margaret sends her love and, of course, cookies. How's it going here?"

"Cynthia, you couldn't have arrived at a better time," Gabrielle said. The relief was obvious in her voice. "Ms. Isabella is in a terrible hurry. Would you help me by stripping the polish off the left hand while I work on the right?"

Kara was relieved when Cynthia answered. "Absolutely. I was only gone a week but I missed you." She then picked up a cotton ball and directed her attention to stripping polish. When she spoke again, it was in French. "Anything exciting happen in my absence, like ah, how did that date turn out?"

"Oh, my!" Gabrielle answered, in French.

Unbeknownst to Gabrielle and Cynthia, Kara understood their communication as Gabrielle began relating the intimate details of her date with a United States Senator by the name of Mark. Although she did not mention Mark's last name, it was obvious to Kara that it was Mark Langford, her fiancé. Kara and Mark had been secretly engaged for three months and were involved in an intimate relationship. Kara had every right to

expect that she and Mark were exclusive. She had
no reason to think otherwise—until now.

As Kara sat there listening to Gabrielle's
detailed rendition of her date with Mark, apparently not their first date, Kara was convinced
Gabrielle was not making up the story. Gabrielle
regaled Cynthia with details of the evening including her intimacy with Mark. Kara recognized the
modes operandi and was instantly consumed with
fury. She inadvertently jerked her hand.

"Did I hurt you?" Gabrielle asked as Kara
clinched her fist and cast daggers in Gabrielle's
direction.

She realized that Gabrielle was not the villain
but a victim just like herself. Kara managed to say
as she gritted her teeth, "I cringed thinking about
all I have to do when I get back to work. It's not
anything you've done."

Kara focused on the real culprit and how she
would exact her pound of flesh. Revenge was in
Kara's DNA, and it stemmed back as far as back
went. Her ancestors were ruthless, and the gene
pool had not been diluted over the centuries. Her
blood ran hot with passion–both love and hate.
There was a fine line between the two. Hate dominated and consumed her soul.

Barely breathing, Kara listened to Gabrielle's
description of her date and finally had to accept
the fact that she had been duped by a master
deceiver. *But what Mark didn't know was that you
don't deceive an Isabella and get away with it. How
dare him use me and Daddy, how dare him! Oh, my
God, I'm too embarrassed to tell Daddy. He would*

have Mark killed. . .I want to do that myself. Perhaps Mark's mantra, what you don't know won't hurt you, could hurt him—very badly. As far as Kara was concerned, Mark's aspirations would be buried with him.

HAVE YOUR CAKE AND EAT IT TOO

MARK'S UNFAITHFULNESS rankled her. Kara's first inclination was to despoil his reputation and undermine his bid for the White House. She liked the idea. *He needs to feel the pain of being deceived, the same pain I'm feeling now.* Suddenly Kara's vision blurred, her heart pounded wildly, her cheeks flushed and her hands began to shake. For a fleeting minute, she thought she was in the throes of cardiac arrest.

"Ma'am, are you feeling alright?" the elevator operator asked.

"I'm okay. I just feel a little faint."

When the elevator stopped at the eleventh floor, she asked, "Can I help you to your suite?"

"I'll be alright. Thank you anyway." Kara was still reeling from the stark realization that she was nothing more than a means to an end. *Who wouldn't succumb to Mark's charms? He's handsome, intelligent, has political standing that renders him even more desirable, and he's fun to be with. People gravitate toward him. If only they knew his dark side. He keeps that devil well hidden. How long did he think he would have his cake and eat it, too? Is he so conceited, he didn't think he'd ever be caught? And I fell for him and his shameful scheme. If I forgive and forget, shame on me!*

Kara was conflicted over breaking up with Mark but knew a lasting relationship was not meant to be. She considered not attending the White House dinner that evening knowing that Mark was expected to attend. If she went, she knew she would have to improvise and give an Academy Award winning performance to keep him from detecting that anything was awry. *I'm not sure I can control my emotions, only that I must.*

Kara locked the door to her office and slumped in the chair at her desk. She pushed her work aside spilling some on the floor. Disgusted and frustrated, she scattered everything that remained so that her office looked like a tornado had struck. Resting her head on her arms, she was awash with feelings of despair and betrayal. She was devastated but not destroyed. After all, *she was an Isabella* and had learned at a very tender age that treachery and deceit begets treachery and deceit. The fact that he would be running for President prompted Kara to reign in her desire for immediate retaliation and wait until the opportunity presented itself. She didn't know when that would occur, only that it would.

Having a plan of sorts, Kara felt better. She dried her eyes, stood, adjusted her jacket, and opened her door. She was ready for business as usual. She could and would face Mark and perpetrate her own brand of deception. If anything, she would probably overcompensate in order not to alert him of her true feelings. He wasn't the only one who could play the game. Before she left for the day, she tidied her office, grateful no one had observed either her temper or the results thereof.

Arriving at the White House, Ambassador Madrid and his party were greeted by a butler who held open the double doors leading into the foyer and ballroom beyond. The ambassador and his wife, Alejandra, entered followed immediately by Kara.

Kara, wearing a gown of white chiffon with a long sweeping skirt, stood on the steps leading to the ballroom allowing the ambassador and Alejandra to go first. Kara never just entered a room, she captivated it. From her vantage point, she could survey the entire venue and immediately spotted Mark, handsome and deceptive in his black tuxedo and chatting with a trio of secretaries from the embassy. *Of course*, she mused, *he never missed a chance to flirt with a skirt.*

The ambassador caught her eye signaling that she should accompany him. Smiling, Kara gracefully descended the steps and sashayed into the ballroom taking her place next to the ambassador and his wife.

Mark looked in Kara's direction and smiled. Plunging his hands into his pants pockets, he stretched and strutted in Kara's direction. Just as he arrived, a waiter breezed by holding a tray shoulder high, and Kara reached up and helped herself to a glass of champagne.

"That was graceful and don't we look ravishing," Mark chirped.

"Why, thank you my sweet. I could say the same thing about you." Sarcasm oozed from Kara's lips as she sipped the champagne. How easy it would be to beat Mark at his own game.

"Well then, why don't you?" Mark teased oblivious to Kara's mood.

"You certainly don't need me to stroke your ego. Looks like you've already started collecting treasures for your harem."

"Do I detect a note of jealousy?"

"Me? Are you kidding? Me? Jealous of *you*? That'll be the day."

Kara noticed Mark rub the back of his neck and frown slightly. He finally said, "What's troubling you?"

Kara hadn't intended to sound so caustic.

Mark's eyes narrowed and he raised his eyebrows.

Kara smiled up at him hoping she hadn't exposed too much and winced when Mark wrapped his arm around her waist, pulling her close. He kissed her on the forehead.

As the reality of it all set in, Kara feared she would collapse and expose her charade. In the presence of Mark, she second-guessed her decision and for a moment thought forgiveness might be an option. Just then Gabrielle's face appeared on her mental screen and the thought of reconciliation became history. She put on her game face, straightened her shoulders, and nudged Mark away. His surprised look delighted her. *It's not*

*Mark who is in control, it's me. If Mark hurts me
again, it will be my fault, not his.*

Having successfully passed the first dreaded
encounter with Mark, Kara actually enjoyed the
dinner. She was seated in what was considered
a place of honor between the ambassador and
United States President Winston F. Warrington
and was blitzed with looks of envy from other
guests. Leaning forward, the President engaged
Kara in a personal conversation and they nodded
and laughed as though they were old friends sharing a private joke. Onlookers might have thought
they were old acquaintances as easy and relaxed as
they were with each other. This isn't so bad after
all, Kara thought as she continued to shun Mark.

During the course of the evening, Kara sur-
reptitiously watched Mark as he wove his web
of enchantment around the female attendees.
She was seeing him with new eyes. Yesterday, she
thought she was head-over-heels in love with him.
Today she loathed him. *Can love change to hate
that quickly?* Her mind drifted as she relived the
days and nights she spent with Mark. *I'm ashamed
of the way I poured myself out on him. He probably
knows me better than I know myself— except for how
ruthless I can be.*

Although it was only ten o'clock, President
Warrington rose and signaled the official end to
the festivities. The president took Kara's hand.
"And, a special thanks to you, my dear, for making
the evening so lively and entertaining."

"Mr. President, the pleasure was all mine. I thoroughly enjoyed the evening especially our dinner discussion. I can understand why the United States is such a prosperous country."

"I look forward to our next encounter, Ms. Isabella. Until then, I bid you a good evening." President Warrington, surrounded by secret service personnel, departed through a private entrance.

As Kara left the dining room, Mark fell in beside her.

"Well, that was quite a performance," Mark said, slipping his arm around her waist. "I didn't know you knew the President. May I take you home?"

"No, thank you. I'm with the ambassador and Alejandra. Maybe we can see each other tomorrow?" Kara slipped from his grasp as Mark stood with a scowl on his face.

"Of course. Why would you even ask?" Mark managed to say.

"Oh, I don't know. You looked like a busy little boy gathering all the pretty flowers in the garden."

"Kara, what is the matter with you? You're acting pretty strange. Did I do something to offend you?" Kara deftly dodged his questions and his attention. "I think I'm just tired. Oh, look, the ambassador is signaling me that they're ready to leave. Talk to you tomorrow."

As Kara turned to leave, Mark attempted to plant the traditional kiss on her cheek, but she quickly turned away. Kara looked around in time to see Mark's dejected expression as he stood with his arms folded.

Kara didn't know how long Mark stood there. She just knew he deserved to be left behind.

🦢

Mark was a cunning individual. He had the gift of sensing what people were thinking and feeling by studying them over a period of time and mentally cataloging their facial expressions, conversation and, of course, moods. *My instincts tell me my relationship with Kara has disintegrated. Everything seemed to be normal up until tonight.* Mark frowned and shook his head. He bid good evening to those around him and left the White House feeling rejection, resentment and resignation.

🦢

Since Kara had given him the brush-off, Mark called Gabrielle. The night was young and Mark knew Gabrielle would be warm and loving—something he desperately needed, especially this night. Mark rated his friends first by their wealth, second by their status and, finally, by what they could do *for* him. Gabrielle fell into the last category.

Gabrielle answered the phone on the first ring.

"Hey you! Are you up to having some company this evening?" he asked, knowing what the answer would be.

"Why, yes. Where are you?"

"I'm just leaving the White House. I can be there in less than two hours."

"Perfect! Cynthia is spending the night with a classmate catching up on assignments she missed while she was in Vermont."

Mark knew Gabrielle wanted him to know they could spend the entire night together alone. It was just the therapy he needed. The diversion provided by Gabrielle would more than compensate for Kara's cold shoulder.

"I'll be there in a jiffy!" Mark didn't say goodbye. He closed his cell phone and left Gabrielle hanging.

Awaiting Mark's arrival, Gabrielle took a quick shower and put on a pale pink negligee. It was Mark's favorite. The gossamer fabric revealed the beautiful curves of her body and the supple mounds of her ample breasts. She pinned her hair up in a jeweled clip that could be removed with a flick of the wrist, reapplied her makeup, and lightly sprayed Chanel No 5 on her neck and shoulders. From the time Gabrielle could remember, Chanel No 5 was the epitome of perfume. Her mother always wore it. The olfactory nerve excites the memory portion of the brain and, as Gabrielle inhaled the fragrance, wonderful thoughts of her mother came pouring back. Even to this day, almost twenty years after her parents' tragic deaths, Gabrielle still missed them terribly. *How different my life might have been if they hadn't been killed.*

Pushing melancholy memories aside, Gabrielle lit some candles and placed them strategically throughout the apartment. She checked the refrigerator to ensure Mark's favorite wine was cooled then cut some cheese wedges and arranged them with crackers and grapes on a crystal platter. Turning 360 degrees, she surveyed the room and was satisfied with the ambiance. Suddenly the doorbell rang. She hurried to the door and swung it open, welcoming Mark inside. He draped his tux jacket over a chair and purred as he gathered her into his arms and pulled her close. "You look marvelous, darling."

She smiled seductively and pulled away. Twirling so that the negligee freely swung around her womanly shape, she answered, "For your eyes only."

"Bet you say that to all your lovers," Mark replied as he gently fingered the small pale pink swan embroidered at the V neckline of the sexy garment.

"Yes, I do. But, since you're my only lover, it's a moot point, don't you think?"

Mark laughed a deep throaty laugh, encircled her waist with his arms, and pulled her to him once more, kissing her passionately. The wine and cheese languished as the two lovers satisfied their longing. Thoughts of Kara quickly vanished as Mark immersed himself in a sea of sexual pleasure. He spent most of the night with Gabrielle and didn't return to Washington until after five the next morning. When he opened his door, he saw the red blinking light on his answering machine and cursed under his breath. He ignored its demands, collapsed onto his unmade bed, and fell into a deep carefree slumber.

Kara was furious when Mark hadn't answered the telephone the third time she called, which was sometime around 1:30 a.m. *That two-timing bastard! How dare he use Daddy and me like this. It's obvious he's with another woman, probably Gabrielle.* In a fit of rage, she threw her phone across the room followed by a vase and a crystal figurine Mark had bought her shortly after they met. *Ah, even if I'd been inclined to forgive and forget, his actions tonight pretty much seal his fate. She pondered the ways she would make Mark pay for his indiscretions. He would get as good as he gave.*

CHAPTER 6

All's Fair in Love and War

HAVING HAD TIME TO CONSIDER the situation, Kara determined she still had strong feelings for Mark, and she needed to have her suspicions confirmed. She was at a point where she didn't know what to believe and didn't want to throw away her chance to marry Mark and become First Lady if her suspicions were incorrect. *After all, Langford isn't the only Senator named Mark. I should have him followed and find out if, when, and where the lovebirds meet. If I get verification, I can proceed with Plan B—whatever that is. One step at a time, there's no cause to rush to judgment. Since we're engaged, I have a right to know what he's up to.*

Early the next morning, which was Saturday, Kara rummaged through her desk and found the notebook containing telephone numbers of some of her father's contacts, contacts that her father had given her before she left Spain. Turning the pages, she was uncertain as to whom she could trust to follow Mark so she telephoned her father for advice.

"Hi Daddy, how are you?"

"Kara! What a wonderful surprise. We were just talking about you."

"What a coincidence, I was just thinking about the two of you as well."

"That's good to hear. How are things in the Large Apple?"

"Just fine, Daddy, but it's the Big Apple, not the Large Apple." Kara didn't waste time but got straight to the point. "Remember, before I left home you gave me a notebook with some names and numbers of contacts in case I ever needed help. You told me you hired someone years ago to watch some key figures here in New York. I don't remember who you recommended. Can you recall his name?"

"Let me think. . . ." Snapping his fingers, her father said, "His name is Vernon, Vernon Simson. Hold on, I'll. . .I'll get you his telephone number." Kara could hear her father flip through his cards. "His number is 970-241-9032."

Kara wrote the telephone number down and said, "You're an angel, Daddy. Thank you."

Kara's father was silent for a long moment.

"Are you there?" Kara asked anxiously.

"Just worried, is all. Hope the surveillance is for romantic reasons and not something more sinister."

"Nothing for you and Mother to get excited about. When things quiet down, I'll tell you all about it."

Later that day Kara went to the mall and purchased a cheap cell phone with prepaid minutes that she would use to contact Simson. *I don't like doing this, but how else can I be sure? I hope this guy is still in business. Guess I'll soon find out.* After purchasing the phone, Kara went to Café Court, sat at an isolated table, and dialed the number her father had provided.

Simson had been an undercover cop with the NYPD and had learned his trade well. He also had retained his contacts from his days of being a cop. It came in handy when he left the force and became a private investigator. He kept busy with warring political candidates and jealous spouses. His PI job more than paid the bills.

"Vern here," a gruff voice boomed in her ear.

"Vernon Simson?"

"Yep, one and the same. Who's asking?"

"You've done work for an acquaintance of mine in the past and come highly recommended," Kara said as she looked around not wanting anyone to hear her conversation. "I'm looking for someone with surveillance skills. Do you still engage in that line of work?"

"Depends."

"Depends? Depends on what exactly?" Kara switched the phone to her other ear. She reached into her purse, fumbling for a pen and note pad.

"Depends on how you answer these two questions: First, will the assignment get me thrown in the slammer? Second, can you afford my services?"

"First of all, this is not a slammer assignment. It is basic surveillance. If you're as good as I've been led to believe, the chances of you getting caught are slight to none. Secondly, I need some kind of dollar figure."

"I'll take your word that the job is legit, but I'll need a five thousand dollar retainer fee upfront. After you tell me exactly what it is you need, I can give you a better estimate of total fees and costs. We need to meet face-to-face and discuss the details. I don't trust phones."

"Will you give me your word that you will keep whatever we discuss confidential?"

"You got it, lady. I learned long ago not to be mouthy—bad for your health in my line of work."

"That's reassuring. When and where do you want to do the face-to-face?"

"No time like the present. Where ya callin' from?"

"Flishman's Mall."

"I'm in the middle of a report. It may take an hour or so. Meet me at one of the tables outside Shelly's Diner 'round two; I'll be wearin' jeans and a white Yankee T-shirt."

When Simson opted to meet right away, Kara almost panicked. *I need a disguise. I don't want him to know who I am. Oh, my God, how can I do this?*

Regaining control, she rushed out into the shopping area of the mall and purchased a red wig and some cheap hooker-style clothing. Kara had a makeup kit in her handbag, so after making the purchases, she went into the women's restroom and donned the new clothing. She applied heavy, sleazy makeup, hoping her disguise was adequate to keep her identity secret.

After making the transition, Kara looked around for the nearest bank in anticipation of hiring Simson on the spot. She was eager to have answers. Locating a branch of her bank midway down the main mall corridor, she withdrew five thousand dollars in cash. Observing the suspicious look the teller threw her way and the harsh demand for identification, Kara thought, *Bitch, I don't care what you think.* Kara snatched the envelope containing the cash from the teller's hand and crammed it into her purse. By the time she arrived back at Café Court, she was out of breath. She stopped long enough to purchase a soft drink from a vending machine before heading for Shelly's Diner. The cafe was easily identifiable with its checkerboard façade. Kara took a seat at one of the tables outside the restaurant where she could easily observe the traffic coming and going. She barely became situated when she noticed a rugged but good-looking, tall, muscular man dressed in jeans, boots, and a white Yankees T-shirt casually swagger into the area. *That has to be him.* The rugged stranger walked past the various businesses, peering in the windows and taking his time much to Kara's chagrin. *It's obvious he doesn't give a damn whether he's on time or not.* When Simson was a few feet from her, their eyes met and both smiled.

"Well, well, what have we here?" he smirked as he looked her over.

Kara was insulted by his remark but didn't let it show. "So, Mr. Simson, why don't you take a seat?"

Simson looked around before seating himself.

"Would you like to go inside the diner and get something to eat or drink?" Kara asked.

"Naw, don't have much time. Ya bring my retainer?"

"Yes."

"Okay. Let's talk turkey. Who is it you want me to tail?"

"A friend. I suspect he's having an affair. However, I don't want to jump to conclusions and make unjustified assumptions."

Simson raised his eyebrows. He said, "A week of simple surveillance will cost you ten Gs plus expenses."

"Sure." Kara sucked in her breath. *Holy crap, ten thousand dollars for a week's surveillance?*

"I'll need his address, a description of the guy and what he drives. Also, your name and contact information?"

"You don't need to know who I am. My money is good. That's all you need to know. Here's a pen—you can use this napkin to take down the information."

"Keep it." He took a pen and small notepad from his shirt pocket. "Shoot."

"His name is Mark Langford and he is a United States Senator and lives at the Keystone in DC. He drives a late model black Cadillac. I don't know the license number. He is chauffeured occasionally and often takes the Acela Express to New York as he is chair of the committee working with the Spanish Embassy at the UN."

"Hold on there! You didn't tell me the target was high profile and I would have to get a place in DC to do the job. That's upping the ante quite a bit," Vern said, tapping the pen on the table.

"How much is quite a bit?" Kara asked. She had come this far, and she was willing to pay the price, whatever it was.

"I think we should renegotiate—fifteen, plus expenses," Vern said, still tapping.

"That is half again what we agreed upon. How about twelve and expenses?"

"Nope. Fee is firm, take it or leave it," Vern tossed the pen down and rose from his seat.

"Okay, okay." Kara fumbled around in her purse and came up with the envelope containing the five thousand dollars.

"Here's your retainer, Mr. Simson. What would be a good time for us to get in touch with each other?"

"Just call me Vern. Can't rightly say. Is the Senator usually home at night?"

"Since I suspect he's having an affair, wouldn't you think he would be out at night?"

"Yeah, right, that makes sense." Vern's face reddened. "Why don't you call me on my cell 'round nine? Here's the number." He handed Kara his card. "I'll be 'specting your call—I keep my phone on vibrate so it doesn't ring. If I don't answer, try back every thirty minutes. I may be in a sensitive situation. Kapish?"

Again Kara was irritated by Simson's casual attitude, but she surmised her cheap disguise warranted little respect. She didn't want to alienate him.

"Yeah, I kapish." And so the plan was set into motion. *I'll have answers within a week, I hope. No matter what, at least I'll know for certain one way or another.* She went home and stored her disguise in a box at the back of her closet. She proceeded through the rest of the day in as normal a fashion as possible.

Mark called her later that afternoon. "Hey you, what's up?"

Kara thought that was pretty casual considering he probably spent the night with another woman. "Same-ole-same-ole. What are you doing?"

"I'm in the office right now and thought you may want to have dinner tonight. I've heard that new place, *Brandon's*, over on 73rd is very good. How 'bout it?"

"Are you in your DC office or your New York office?" Kara thought of his past actions and all the impromptu dinner meetings with his *committee* that he would suddenly spring on her. Then, as if to make amends for his infidelity, he would hurriedly include an invitation to take her to dinner the next evening. To his way of thinking, that would make up for his philandering. So, true to his established pattern, this was the expected dinner invitation.

"I'm in DC but plan on taking the train to New York later this afternoon if you agree to have dinner with me."

"Sure, why not. Will seven o'clock work for you?" Kara could barely hide the contempt in her voice.

"Yes. I should be in New York by five this afternoon. I'll call when I arrive to firm up our plans."

"Okay. See you later." Kara hung up without saying goodbye. *I hope that hurt his feelings—but then, he would have to have feelings in order for them to be hurt.*

As Kara was getting ready for dinner, she was secure in the knowledge that Vern would be on the job. *I might even catch a glimpse of him doing his job but maybe not. He's supposed to be a master of disguise.*

🦢

Mark arrived in New York close to five and telephoned Kara.

"Shall I come get you?" Kara offered.

"No need. I'll grab a cab and meet you at *Brandon's* at seven."

The restaurant was on the twentieth floor of the Fieldbrook Hotel. Mark was first to arrive and was shown to a table positioned close to a bank of windows. The two glass walls offered an amazing panorama of the New York skyline. Sitting there looking around while he waited for Kara, Mark wondered, *How much is this little escapade is going to cost me?*

🦢

Disguised as an old man with thick glasses and a cane, Simson followed Mark into the lobby and overheard him ask a bell captain for directions to *Brandon's*. Simson surmised Mark was meeting someone, so knowing Mark's destination, he went back to the parking garage. From a safe vantage point, he recorded the license plate numbers of all the solo women who entered and took photographs with his cell phone of each babe as she exited her vehicle.

Vern slouched against a BMW parked close to the entrance. As he loitered there organizing his notes, a snappy little fire-engine-red T-bird tore into the garage and screeched to a halt straddling two parking slots. The vanity plate, HT-U-NO-WT, caught his attention. *Well, now, what have we here?* He jotted the license plate number down. When the driver exited the vehicle, Vern grimaced. *Good Lord! That chick definitely needs a gimmick. Hope her john has a strong constitution.* He quickly recorded her license number and took her photograph. Next to the license number, he wrote "coyote ugly."

Vern looked at his watch and decided it was time to join the happy couple. When he entered *Brandon's*, he took a seat at the bar and ordered a beer. He could see Mark and his date in the mirrored wall behind the bar. He recognized the woman sitting with Mark as belonging to one of the license numbers he had recorded on his notepad. To Mark's credit, it was not the woman Vern tabbed "coyote ugly."

Mark looked up as Kara approached their table and sucked in his breath at the sight of her. Kara took special care to look her very best. She wore the quintessential LBD. With her long dark hair piled high and three-inch heels enhancing her shapely legs, she looked irresistible. Straight out of *Vogue*, he thought as the maître d' held her chair. She gracefully slipped onto it.

"You look ravishing, darling," Mark whispered.

"Why, thank you," she whispered back.

Within a short time, the waiter approached and presented Mark with a list of wine selections. Not looking at the list, Mark ordered a bottle of

Barefoot White Zen, their favorite from their first date two years ago.

"Is my selection to your liking?" Mark whispered to Kara.

"It's my favorite for several reasons," Kara whispered back. "By the way, why are we whispering?"

"No reason. It just seems more intimate. Now tell me why Barefoot's your favorite."

"Mainly, the taste," Kara teased.

"And I thought it was because Barefoot marked our first date."

"Oh, I forgot," Kara said as Mark glowered.

Picking up the menu, Mark said, "I'm looking at the prime rib. With no lunch, I could eat a horse. How 'bout you?"

"Not into meat tonight, especially not horse. What is the seafood entrée this evening?"

"H-m-m-m, let's see. Oh, here it is, grilled tuna steak."

"Perfect, I'll have that, a baked potato, and salad," Kara answered. "Would you order for me while I powder my nose?"

"Sure. Don't take too long, I'm already missing you."

Kara smiled sweetly as she rose and walked toward the ladies' room. Every eye in the room, male and female alike, watched as she sashayed past. *Look at the way men leer at the little whore. I have no idea what's bothering her. I'm getting tired of trying to please the bitch. If it weren't for Daddy's money and influence. . .*

Kara returned to the table just as the waiter was serving the salad. Mark was in the process of pouring the wine.

"I ordered house dressing for both of us. Hope that suits you." Mark then offered a toast. "May love always triumph!"

"May love triumph!" Kara replied as the two clicked their glasses together.

"I detect a slight cold front moving through. Is it the weather or something I've done?"

"Why, Mark. You sound like a man with a guilty conscience," Kara smirked as she daintily spread butter on a dinner roll. "What have you been up to?"

"Aww, come on Kara. You know what I'm talking about. We've been together long enough that we know each other pretty well. I can tell when there's something going on in that pretty little head of yours."

"Really? Now you're a mind reader?"

"Okay, we'll play it your way. You've been giving me the cold shoulder. What did I do to upset you?" Mark twisted the wine glass between his thumb and forefinger. "I can't do this cat-and-mouse gig. If you're not going to tell me, how can I make amends?"

"Oh, Mark, let's not quibble and spoil such a lovely dinner."

Mark shrugged his shoulders. He picked up his fork and attacked his salad. "Anything you say, my pet. May I pour you more wine?" *If I get her tipsy, she may loosen up and tell me what's bothering her.*

Mark refilled Kara's wine glass, all the while studying her face. When she picked up her glass, he noticed her nails. He choked on a bite of salad. Mark instantly had a flash back to the first time Gabrielle had given him a manicure. He remembered she said, "Let me paint my trademark on your right pinky." It was a tiny pink swan. Now looking at the tiny swan on Kara's right pinky, it hit him, *Oh, my God! Kara found out about Gabrielle.*

"Are you all right?" Kara asked.

Mark indicated with the wave of his hand that he was all right. He coughed into his napkin and wiped tears from his eyes. "Well," he gasped, "that was a very vinegary bite. That's what I get when I gulp down my food."

"You had me worried." Kara was intent on watching the other diners wondering if Vern might already be on the job.

The rest of the dinner continued in virtual silence. Mark had lost his appetite but forced himself to eat to keep Kara from suspecting he knew her secret. *Damn it, if I lose Kara, I lose it all. Look at the smug little bitch. I suppose she's reveling in the knowledge that I'm suffering because of her little charade. I wonder if she knows the significance of the pink swan. I doubt it; otherwise she would have removed it before meeting me.* After the initial shock and choking episode, he regained his composure. Mark had thick skin. He prided himself on being the consummate politician.

"Are you staying in New York or taking the train back to DC?" Kara asked over coffee and dessert.

"Well, that's up to you. I was hoping we could spend the weekend together. I brought a few things." He pointed to the small duffel bag he had sitting on the empty chair.

"Oh, I'm so sorry, Mark. I have plans for the weekend. You should have said something sooner."

After signing the receipt and placing the credit card in his wallet, Mark rose and held Kara's chair.

"Don't forget your duffel," Kara said in a sugary tone. Mark picked up the bag and the two headed for the exit.

Vern had been watching, and he managed to arrive at the elevators first. He was standing in front of one of the elevators in his disguise when Mark and the woman approached and the door slid open. He rode down with them. When the good-looking gal spoke to Mark in the elevator, Vern recognized her voice from their meeting at the mall. *Well, well, ain't that just hunky-dory. Gotcha. It won't be long before I know who you are. The Internet is a godsend. Nothing is sacred anymore.*

When they left the hotel, the couple stood in awkward silence under the green canvas awning covering the walkway outside the Fieldbrook. Vern pretended to wait for a cab.

"I'll call you tomorrow," Mark said.

"Sure," came the woman's reply. She sounded distant and cold.

Vern watched as they parted with a hug and a traditional quick peck on the cheek.

⤳

Mark's first inclination was to call Gabrielle and immediately end the affair. Then he supposed that calling her would be much too cold. He had to do it in person.

⤳

Vern observed Mark fish his cell phone from his jacket pocket with one hand while clutching his duffel with the other. He watched as Mark hastened down the boulevard. After a brief phone conversation, he saw Mark flag down a cabbie. Vern had been in the business far too long not to have planned for that contingency, and he had made arrangements to have his own cab waiting for him as he came out of the hotel. After all, it was his client's money he was spending. When Mark boarded the cab he hailed, Vern jumped into the one he had hired and said, "Follow that cab!" He heard the cabbie mutter, "Oh, shit, not another Bogie wanna-be."

⤳

At the end of the ride, Vern paid the driver. While Mark was fumbling with his wallet, Vern entered the lobby of the Brookline apartments. He pretended to be looking for a name on the mailboxes as Mark came in and shot through the lobby straight to the elevators. Vern snapped his fingers as though he had found the party he was searching for and hurried to the elevator. The elevator stopped on the fourth floor and both men got off. Vern looked up and down the long

corridor with a perplexed expression on his face.
Mark headed for the far end of the hallway. The
door opened and an attractive female stood in the
doorway wearing a pink gossamer negligee. Vern
guessed the woman to be in her early twenties.
After the door closed, the lock snapped. He took
note of the apartment number, stepped back onto
the elevator and descended to the first floor. Vern
was whistling a tune as he matched the names to
the apartment number on the mailbox and swag-
gered toward the exit proud of his accomplish-
ment. Once outside, he flagged another cab. He'd
take the Acela Express back to DC to pick up his
car where he had left it when he followed Mark
to the station earlier that evening. Good Lord, the
entire caper only took seven days and he made fifteen Gs, plus expenses. *Not bad for a week's work,*
he thought as he leaned his head back against the
worn leather seat. *Beats my salary at the NYPD.*

๛

"Mark, I'm so glad you could make it," Gabrielle said as she threw her arms around Mark's
neck and pressed her body close to his, kissing
him passionately.

God, how am I going to do this? Mark thought.
I was so distracted after determining Kara knew
about Gabrielle I didn't think it through.

"As always, you look enchanting," Mark managed to mutter as Gabrielle took his bag to the
bedroom.

*I can't just dump her; she could ruin me. She has
connections through the spa. I need to think this thing*

*through. Maybe just one more romp in the sack for old
times' sake.*

"I can only stay a couple of hours. I have a
meeting with my committee early in the morning," Mark said, trying to find an excuse.

"Are you meeting on a Sunday?" Gabrielle
asked.

"Why, yes." Mark realized he'd been caught in
a lie. "The bill we're working on will be on the
floor first thing Monday, and we have to hammer
out some details. Didn't I mention that?"

"No."

"I'm sorry, I thought I told you. Let's not waste
what time we have," Mark said and pulled her
close. *This evening will be our swan song.* Mark
slipped the spaghetti straps down Gabrielle's
shoulders, allowing the negligée to flutter to the
floor. He would have to improvise to justify his
change of plans. Duty required that he spend the
night.

CHAPTER 7

AGAINST THE MIDDLE

THE NEXT DAY VERN prepared a report for Kara detailing the events of the previous evening, which included the appearance of a beautiful woman who met Langford at the Fieldbrook Hotel for dinner. *I'd rather that pompous bitch not know I'm on to her. Who knows how valuable that knowledge could be in the future?* Just as he was finishing up the paperwork, his phone rang.

"Simson." he answered in a gruff voice.

"This is your current employer. Do you have anything significant yet?"

"Yes, ma'am, I do. I just finished my report. Do you want to meet at the same place?"

"Yes," Kara answered.

"Bring the rest of the moola plus an additional fifteen to cover expenses?"

"I will have it by the time we meet." Kara said. "You seem pretty confident you have the information I requested."

"Indeed I do." Vern answered. "What's a good time to meet since you're the one with the errand to run?"

"I can get it together in an hour."

"Roger, see you in an hour."

Kara hung up the phone. Her heart beat like a humming bird's wings. In some ways, she hoped her suspicions would be confirmed. In other ways, she wished it were just the opposite. Regardless, she could adjust to either.

After donning her previous disguise, Kara drove to the bank and withdrew fifteen thousand dollars in cash. She tried to ignore the looks and whispers of the tellers as they scrambled to get the money together. Kara looked over her shoulder at the line that was forming behind her and ignored the angry looks directed her way. She repeatedly checked her watch as she drummed her fingers on the counter. When, at last, she was handed a banker's bag containing the cash, she whirled and, almost knocking over the woman behind her, tore out of the bank, leaving in her wake stunned tellers and disgruntled customers.

Kara drove recklessly down the busy streets barely avoiding serious accidents in her rush to get to the mall. She saw Vern sitting at a table drinking a soda. As she walked up, he gestured for her to sit. Kara watched as Vern removed a folder from the valise he had brought with him and said, "You got the dough?"

"It's right here," Kara responded, handing him an envelope. She watched him fan through the stack of bills and, when he finished, he handed her his report.

"I can't read this now." She folded the report and put it in her purse.

Striding through the parking lot, Kara was conflicted. She wasn't sure she even wanted to read the report. In her heart, she knew what it said. However, once inside her Audi, she could stifle her curiosity no longer. *Just as I suspected. I'm not surprised—heartbroken—but not crushed.* She read the part about Gabrielle answering the door in a pink negligee. Disappointment turned to rage. Hot tears streamed down her cheeks as she pondered what could have been.

Kara suppressed her anger and forced herself to remain calm. She drove home and shed the disguise. After taking a shower, she inserted her favorite CD into the stereo, poured herself a glass of wine, and settled back on the oversized sofa. She let her mind drift. Her reverie was interrupted by the phone ringing. *That's probably Mark. I can't talk to him now—maybe never, that deceitful, lying, rat bastard.* Another barrage of tears filled her eyes, and she buried her head in the sofa pillows. Finally, Kara fell into a deep sleep.

The next morning she awakened to an overcast sky that mirrored her mood, dark and gloomy. *My God, how much wine did I drink?* Her head pounded like a jungle drum. Two empty bottles sitting on the kitchen counter provided the answer. Kara retrieved Vern's report from the coffee table. The ink was smeared with wine stains comingled with tears. She studied the report more carefully and in a fit of rage tore it into a thousand tiny pieces. *I'm an Isabella, not a whiny schoolgirl. I'm in control of my destiny and, after this revelation, Mark's fate as well. There is a price to pay for every indiscretion, and*

*I will make sure that Mark's indiscretion is repaid
ten-fold.*

🦢

Gabrielle looked forward to Monday not
merely because it was her day off from work, but
because that was the day Mark usually appeared
on the scene. She wondered if maybe he was
thinking about a more permanent relationship
and was about to propose. She was in love with
him and sure that he loved her as well.

🦢

Mark, concerned over the disintegration of his
relationship with Kara, spent the weekend devis-
ing a plan to end his involvement with Gabrielle.
He was feeling very foolish about risking everything with Kara. Now his biggest concern was
how to make it right with her. *Anything I say or do
now will only confirm her suspicions. I need to break
up with Gabrielle before it's too late. Kara is the key
to the fulfillment of my aspirations—not Gabrielle.
Gabrielle is expendable; Kara is not!*

🦢

As usual, Mark took the train to New York that
following Monday. He had worked out a solution
that sounded reasonable to him, and one he hoped
Gabrielle would buy. After all, it was partly true. *I'll
tell her that my party has found out about our affair. The
fact that she is not an American citizen bothers them,
and they will not support my nomination for President
in the next election unless I discard the baggage. The
American people won't tolerate having a foreigner as*

First Lady. I'll plead with her to understand and that if she truly loves me, she won't stand in the way of my fulfilling my dream to be President.

⸜

Gabrielle met Mark at the door. She looked even more radiant than usual. She wrapped her arms around his neck, kissing him passionately on the lips. Mark responded at first but then pushed her away.

"Mark, what is it, darling?"

He turned, walked away from her, and turned back. "Gabrielle, I'm afraid we're going to have to quit seeing each other—at least for a while."

Gabrielle grabbed his hand and looked into his eyes. "But why?"

Mark took a couple of steps back and, rubbing his forehead, shook his head. "I was approached by my campaign manager. There seems to be a problem with me getting closely involved with someone who is not an American citizen and who may be perceived as becoming the First Lady. You know I've been slated to be the party's nominee for President. My party will not back me if they don't think I have a chance to win. I was asked to give you up for the sake of our country and our party. Although it hurts me to do so, I have a greater calling that I must answer."

Gabrielle was stunned. "But, Mark, I love you. . . ."

"I know. And I love you too, but please consider how much this means to me. I know you want what is best for me and my country."

Gabrielle pulled away from him. Mark grabbed for her as she whirled and dashed wildly out onto the balcony. Tears streamed down her cheeks. In her haste, Gabrielle failed to see the wrought-iron table in her path and tripped over it. Attempting to catch her balance, she fell backwards against the balcony railing and toppled over the edge. Mark rushed to grab her but she was beyond his reach. Her scream was abruptly cut off when she slammed onto the pavement below. Mark ran to the railing and peered over the edge. He could see her limp body and watched as a crowd began to gather. He saw a man in the distance look up at him. Mark retreated into the dark shadows of Gabrielle's apartment.

My God, I didn't want it to end like this. Mark was devastated. He was torn between remorse and relief at Gabrielle's sudden demise. *I need to get outta here before all hell breaks loose. What did I touch. . .? The doorknob, anything else?* Mark did a quick sweep around the apartment. He had just barely arrived when the accident occurred, so he was sure there wasn't any evidence that could link him to having been there that afternoon. *I don't have time to sanitize the entire apartment. Just have to take my chances.* He removed his handkerchief from his pants pocket and opened the door. He wiped both sides of the doorknob before setting the lock and exiting the apartment. Instead of taking the elevator, Mark took the stairs. A barrage of emergency personnel would soon appear upon the scene, and he wanted to be as far away as possible. Guilt engulfed him as ran down four stories in the dark narrow staircase to the doorway that opened at the side of the building. *What could I have done differently? The accident wasn't my fault. I had no choice but to break it off with her.* The scream of sirens interrupted his reverie, and he panicked. At all costs, he had to avoid being recognized.

Vern Simson was standing with the crowd of on-lookers when the emergency crew arrived on the scene. He positioned himself at the edge of the crowd and watched the side entrance as well as the rear of the building. His instincts were correct once again when he saw Langford coming out the stairwell exit. *Well, you ole son-of-a-gun. Say cheese. . .* Vern raised his camera and snapped several more pictures. He watched Langford hastily exit the building and look in all directions, hanging in the shadows as EMTs and police personnel descended on the scene.

"Okay, everyone, step back. Give us some room. Go on now, clear the way," a uniformed NYPD officer bellowed over the din of the crowd.

"Coming through," a male nurse with the emergency medical team shouted as he wheeled a gurney onto the sidewalk. It was obvious that there was no need to hurry. Gabrielle had died instantly. The responders were ready to remove the body as soon as the investigators and the medical examiner gave them the go-ahead.

Two uniformed officers, nightsticks in hand, began in earnest to disperse the crowd, so the EMTs could do their job. All the while, Vern kept his eye on Mark and tailed him, stopping only long enough to snap more pictures.

Vern stayed close and watched as Mark hailed a cab. Unable to flag down a cab of his own, Vern gave up the idea of trying to follow Mark. Returning to his Range Rover, Vern was sure what he had captured on film would be money in the bank. At the moment, he wasn't sure how valuable the photographs would be, only that they would be.

It was after five when Mark arrived home. Numb over the events of the afternoon, he escaped to the lounge in his upscale apartment building and sat down at the piano bar. The piano player, with a half empty glass of scotch on the rocks perched on the edge of the keyboard, played a song Mark didn't recognize. The five o'clock crowd had come and gone. The dinner crowd had yet to arrive, so the lounge was empty except for a few hangers-on.

"Mark, you look like a train wreck. Are you okay?" Edwardo, the piano player said after banging out the last cords of his rendition and reaching for his glass.

"What? Oh, yeah. I'm okay. It's just been one of those days."

"Did you enjoy my new number?"

"Didn't hear all of it. What's the title?"

"Don't Give Me Tomorrow."

"You don't have any idea how profound that is. You write it?"

"Nope, wish I could write music like that. It's another Multz composition. Sounds like you're trying to forget someone or something."

"As I just said, you have no idea."

"Can I get you the usual?" the buxom barmaid with too much makeup asked.

"Thought you'd never ask. Bring me a double. No, make that two doubles."

"I didn't want to interrupt."

"I wouldn't have cared if you had."

"One of those days?"

"Yes, one of those days."

When Greta placed the double martini in front of him, Mark just stared at it.

"Not what you wanted?" she asked.

"It's not the drink. I'm just not in the mood for anything."

Mark placed a twenty on the piano next to the untouched drink and headed up to his apartment. He was too weary to turn on the lights. He collapsed on the bed with his arm over his forehead and tried to relax. All he could see behind his eyelids was Gabrielle's flailing arms as she went reeling over the railing.

Kara had just finished her dinner of grilled chicken and salad when she heard Gabrielle LaTana's name coming from a TV news program. She dropped her fork and ran into the living room. The news was being broadcast live from the scene

in front of the Brookline Apartments, and the
cameraman panned the blood stained sidewalk
where LaTana had hit the pavement. The reporter
was saying, "…died at approximately 2:15 this
afternoon after a fall from the fourth floor. Wit-
nesses state they heard a scream and then saw a
young woman falling. Investigators at the scene
are not saying if this was an accident, suicide or
homicide. We will keep you posted as we learn
more…." Kara turned off the news. *What in the
world happened out there? Did Mark push her?"*
Kara immediately telephoned her fiancé.

"Langford!" Mark barked into the phone.

"Mark, you are there! This is Kara. How
are you?" Kara was surprised he answered. She
thought he might still be in New York.

"Uh, fine. Why do you ask? When I last saw
you, you seemed to be ticked off at me for some
inexplicable reason."

"Oh, that. PMS. Have you seen the evening
news?"

"No, why?" Mark asked. "Are we at war?"

"Nothing that drastic. I just saw where one of
the manicurists who worked in the spa near the
UN took a swan dive off her balcony. Her name
was Gabrielle LaTana, and oddly enough, she had
just given me a manicure. She was quite beautiful;
wonder what made her jump. Did you know her?"

Mark hesitated.

"Ah….yes," he finally responded.

"Why the hesitation?" Kara knew Mark didn't
want to admit he knew Gabrielle.

"Oh, I was just trying to remember. She also

manicured my nails on occasion. What a tragedy! Are they saying how it happened?"

"Investigators are being tight-lipped about the circumstances. They still aren't saying if it was an accident, suicide or homicide. Mark, I really feel badly about the tiff we had and would like to make it up to you. Are you free for dinner tomorrow?"

Kara noticed a change in Mark's voice. *He's suspicious of my intentions,* Kara surmised.

Mark said, "Actually, no. I have a previous commitment with my, ah, my committee. We are having dinner catered, so we can address several issues without being disturbed. Why don't I call you later in the week and we can get together if you still want to."

Kara was disappointed. *The old committee meeting ruse again but without Gabrielle this time.*

"Sure. Give me a call." Kara hung up.

Kara sat pondering the recent events when her phone rang. She didn't look at the caller ID because she figured it was Mark trying to schedule dinner. "Yes, what now?" she snapped.

"What now? Well, little lady, you may be in for a big surprise," Vern snapped back.

"Who is this?" she asked.

"I suspect you know who it is. I have something you may be very interested in."

"And what might that be?" Kara sneered.

"I'm the auctioneer and I'm selling to the highest bidder. I have some photographs of the *accident* that happened this afternoon at the Brookline Apartments. Are you interested?"

"What kind of pictures?"

"Pictures of a friend of yours."

"What friend?"

"Now, now, don't get the cart before the horse. I'll email you a sample with a follow up phone call. If you're interested, make me an offer. I have a set of twenty-eight photographs. Just so you know, you're not the only customer I'm considering so make sure the offer isn't insulting."

Kara went immediately to her computer and drummed her fingers on the keyboard, waiting for the mystery email. Not knowing what to expect, she trembled as she opened the file and gasped when she saw the picture of Mark peering over the railing and Gabrielle's crumpled body on the walkway. Wild thoughts raced through her head. *Could it be? Did Mark push Gabrielle off the balcony?* She wanted the other pictures at any price. A few seconds later, the phone rang again.

"Who is this?" she asked.

"Don't you recognize my voice? We've met several times. Are you interested in cutting a deal for the rest of the photographs or not?

"Why should I be?"

"Since you had me following Langford for a week, I thought you might be."

"I did no such thing!" Kara was almost frantic. *How did he know it was me?*

"Come on, now. I recognized your voice in the elevator the evening you had dinner with Langford at *Brandon's* earlier this week. I was the little hunched over mute in the elevator. I got your license plate and the rest is history."

This certainly puts a different slant on things, Kara thought. "Have you contacted anyone else to make an offer?"

"Not yet. Since you're an established client, thought I'd give you first crack at it."

"I'm flattered. How much?"

"Thought I'd let you decide. How bad do you want the photos?"

"How much?" Kara persisted.

"Twenty-five G's."

Kara gasped. She had something like five in mind. "And exactly what do I get for that kind of money?"

"You get the whole enchilada. I didn't see a thing. I wasn't even there."

"How is it you think I'd trust you?"

"That's your problem. My word is my bond. Otherwise, I couldn't survive among my peers and my clientele, if you know what I mean."

Although money's not the problem: I just hate like hell to pay him twenty-five thousand dollars for twenty-eight pictures. That's almost a thousand dollars a photo. But. . .I want them. "Okay, it's a deal. How do you want to proceed with the exchange?"

"Nothing wrong with the routine we used before. But lose the hooker outfit, I have a reputation to maintain. I'll meet you at the usual place tomorrow at three. Does that give you enough time to get the cash together?" Vern asked.

"Yes. That works for me."

"Okay then. See ya tomorrow."

After hanging up the phone, Kara accessed her bank records online. She had $30,000 in her savings account. *How am I going to withdraw twenty-five thousand dollars in cash? That's gotta raise suspicion. There are several branches scattered about town, so maybe by getting an early start I can hit five of them and withdraw five thousand dollars from each. I don't owe anybody an explanation.*

The next morning minus the hooker disguise, Kara left early and went from branch to branch withdrawing five thousand dollars from each. She was scrutinized at a couple locations, probably because of the previous withdrawals. She didn't have time to worry about what the tellers thought, or anyone else for that matter, *Screw 'em!*

At precisely 3:00 p.m., Vern entered the café court at the mall. He spotted Kara sitting at *their* usual table nursing a cup of coffee. When he approached, she jumped. "You startled me," she said.

"Sorry, thought you were expecting me."

"I am. I guess I'm just jumpy carrying this much cash around."

"I can solve that problem." He slid a large envelope across the table. "Here are the photographs. I erased them from my camera and computer. Now you have the only set. I presume from your previous statement you have the cash."

"Yes," Kara said as she slid a shoebox containing the money across the table. She opened the envelope and scanned the photographs, shaking her head in disbelief.

"You're sure I have the only set?" She asked as she examined and re-examined the photographs.

"I wouldn't be in business long or, for that matter alive long, if I weren't true to my word. You do have the only set." Vern opened the shoebox and peered inside. He smiled at the sight of the currency and rifled through it with the experience of someone familiar with handling cash and a lot of it. "Looks like it's all here. Pleasure doing business with you—again. Have a good one." He rose and turned to leave.

"Wait! There is one more thing," Kara blurted.

Vern turned to face her and said, "There are no refunds. Mine is a 'take it as is' business."

"I'm more than pleased with your services. I just need to know how it was you happened to be at the exact location at the precise time Gabrielle fell to her death."

"Trade secret," Vern answered. "Sometimes I'm lucky. Most of the time it's intuition. Yesterday was a combination of both."

"I'm impressed."

"Sure, who wouldn't be? If you need any follow-up, you know where to reach me."

Kara watched Vern's back as he snaked his way through the tables and out the exit. She put the photographs in her handbag and exited the mall. Kara did not know what she was going to do with the photographs. She did know she held all the aces, and there would be a time to play her hand. It mattered not how high the stakes. *The higher the better!* Kara held on tightly to her handbag knowing that it contained the keys to the White House—but not for Mark.

CHAPTER 8

THE PEN IS MIGHTIER
THAN THE SWORD

THE NEXT MORNING after checking the ambassador's calendar, Kara called the Embassy and left word she would be out for the rest of the day. She was allowed liberal comp time as her job description required her to attend the numerous evening functions with the ambassador.

Kara flipped through the news channels, searching for the latest on Gabrielle's death. She found only a blurb to the effect that the investigation was still ongoing. She was curious about whether the authorities had zeroed in on a suspect and whether Mark was in their sights. She didn't dare call the authorities, so she called Mark at his office to ascertain if he knew anything about the investigation.

Maryann, Mark's receptionist, answered the phone. "I'm sorry, Ms. Isabella, Mr. Langford is gone for the day. Would you like to leave a message?"

"Thank you, no, I'll try him at home." Kara was not surprised Mark had made himself scarce. She figured he would be indisposed until the dust settled. He had a way of dodging confrontation and being unavailable at the most inopportune moments.

Mark had played hooky and gone to the gym. *A good workout should clear my head and revive my body.* He was still in a mild state of shock and was finding it difficult to accept the realization of the previous afternoon. *Was it all a bad dream?* He had already convinced himself that what happened to Gabrielle was at her doing and not his. Still, he couldn't remove from his mind the scene of Gabrielle falling to eternity. He closed his eyes and grunted under the strain of the weights. Covered with perspiration, he finally gave it up and went to the locker room. He took a hot shower followed by a cold blast of water. Although he couldn't forget the tragedy, he felt better, at least physically.

"Mark, hey, buddy, where ya been? Haven't seen ya around for awhile." David yelled from the far end of the locker room. Newman was a friend who worked for the FBI.

"Hey, Dave," Mark waved. "I've been swamped and haven't had time to pamper myself and it's beginning to show," Mark said, rubbing his flat stomach. "How 'bout you? Been keeping the criminals at bay?"

"Only when there's a federal connection. Right now we're looking into the death of a young woman thought to have had international ties."

Mark felt the blood drain from his face. "Read about that in the morning paper," he managed to say. "Sounds to me like suicide."

"All I can tell you is that it involves a possible security breach. Our bureau received an anonymous call suggesting that the dead woman had ties with a top government official."

Mark could hardly restrain himself. *I must have been recognized.* The sweat that poured from his brow was not just from the workout. He jammed his arms into his sweatshirt and picked up his gym bag. "Nice seeing ya, Dave. Let's get together for lunch sometime soon."

"Give me a call."

Opening the door to his apartment, Mark noticed the flashing light on his answering machine begging for attention. Kara's message was the first. "Mark, call me when you get this. It's important that I talk to you."

He stabbed at the delete key harder than he intended. *What more do we have to discuss? She's been scarce, now she can stew.* He threw his gym bag toward the closet and flopped down on his bed.

Later that evening, Mark was startled awake by the ringing of the phone. He didn't know how long he had been asleep, but it was dark outside. He took a quick look at the caller ID and then at the clock. *Kara! Doesn't she ever give up? Don't wanna talk to her now—maybe never. She's the reason I'm in this mess. She has a lot of nerve calling me at two in the morning.*

"Mark, I'm worried about you. Please give me a call."

Yeah, she's worried, like I'm about to buy that. She's frantically trying to find out something. Don't much care what she wants. Screw 'er. She'll be furious but then I don't give a damn. Let her call Daddy, I can win the election without his support. Ignoring her recorded plea, he turned over and went back to sleep. He had too much else on his mind than to concern himself with Kara's moods and demands.

Gabrielle's roommate, Cynthia Sawyer, was contacted by the NYPD and asked to come to the police station for an interview. She agreed to do so but was leery of what the police wanted from her. Upon her arrival, she was escorted into Detective Steve Carson's office.

"Hello, Cynthia," Carson said. Did you manage to get some rest?"

"Not much, I was awake all night thinking of Gabrielle."

"I won't keep you long," Carson said. "Just some loose ends. . . ."

"Anything I can do to help," Cynthia replied.

Carson sat at the drab gray steel institutional desk across from Cynthia and looked from her to the form he was filling out as he gathered her personal information. He asked her name, address, occupation, date of birth, place of employment and the name and telephone number of the next of kin.

Cynthia's apprehension mounted as she sat looking around Carson's small sterile office waiting for him to fill out the form. The room was dull green, and five steel filing cabinets lined one wall. Carson had an array of plaques and awards grouped together on the wall behind his desk. It looked as though he had on display every award he had received since his Boy Scout days.

Cynthia wasn't used to the third degree. Since her first interview by the authorities, she had felt guilty about not revealing Mark's true identity. She now felt not only external turmoil but internal turmoil as well. *I don't like the way this feels. I can't throw Senator Langford under the bus. If he killed Gabrielle, what would keep him from killing me, too?*

Steve Carson glanced up. "How long have you known Gabrielle?" he asked, holding the pen poised over the pad in front of him.

"About a year or so. We both worked at the same place in addition to being roommates."

"Had she demonstrated any suicidal tendencies in the recent past that you are aware of?"

"No, none whatsoever. In fact, she was always very upbeat. There was someone special in her life, and she looked forward to each day with hope and expectancy," Cynthia coughed. *Good God, why did I say that?*

Carson tilted his head and squinted. "Do you know who that special someone was?"

"Not really. She just called him by a pet name, err, ah, Honey Bear. She was head over heels over him, if you know what I mean." *How do I get myself into these messes?* Cynthia folded her arms across her chest and wished the interview were over.

She observed Carson's demeanor change as he peered at her. "Yes, I know what you mean. Do you know Honey Bear's legal name or have any other information regarding him?"

"All I know is that they dated. She was a manicurist, and he may have been one of her customers. I don't really know for sure."

Cynthia had made up the name Honey Bear on the spur of the moment. She, of course, knew Mark and had seen and talked with him. Today, loyalty, but mostly fear, kept her from revealing his name. She opted to keep that information to herself. She also knew Mark was being groomed to run for President. The stakes here were extremely high for both of them.

"You wouldn't have a description of him, would you?"

"Only that he was very handsome." *I knew it! I just knew it. I'm going to end up having to betray him or go to jail.*

Tapping the end of his ballpoint against his chin, Carson asked, "Is there anything else you care to add to the information you gave to Detective Alexander yesterday or to me today?" Cynthia shook her head. "Do you know if Gabrielle had any enemies or anyone who would want to do her harm? Simply falling off of a balcony doesn't add up, so we're not calling this an accident until we do a thorough investigation."

"Nothing off-hand. I loved Gabrielle like a sister. Everyone loved her," Cynthia said, trying to hold back the tears.

"Okay, Ms. Sawyer, that's enough for now. We need to get your prints to match with those we collected at the apartment. After that, you're free to leave but if you decide to change residences, you need to let us know. By the way, don't leave town unless you clear it through our department. Guess you've heard that routine before but take it seriously, we mean it."

Detective Carson led Cynthia into the fingerprint alcove where she was printed and released.

He scratched his head as he watched her leave. Returning to his office, he slumped into his hard, well-worn desk chair, shook his head and stared into space.

Cason jerked upright when Dan Alexander entered his office, "Lose your girlfriend?" Alexander asked.

"Where the hell have you been? I thought you were going to sit in on Sawyer's interview?"

"Had to testify in court at the last minute in a juvenile case. How'd the interview go?"

"I think Ms. Sawyer is hiding something or protecting someone."

"Remember me telling you the same thing after I talked to her?"

"She worked with Gabrielle and said Gabrielle's boyfriend 'may have been a customer.' Come now, she didn't know his name and couldn't describe what he looked like. How stupid does she think we are?"

"Do you think she did it?"

"Whoever did it didn't leave prints behind. The knobs on the door were wiped. If the roommate did it, she wouldn't have worried about leaving prints behind."

"Whether Gabrielle was pushed or fell, whoever wiped the prints knew what they were doing and obviously didn't want to hang around long enough to have to explain what happened."

"There's no motive for the roommate to have committed the act. Besides, she had a solid alibi. According to her co-workers, she was at work at the time of Gabrielle's death."

"There was no evidence that Gabrielle was ill or had left work early to catch up on her sleep. Wearing a nightgown would make one suspect it had something to do with her boyfriend."

"The fact that there was no evidence of a struggle or anything out of the ordinary would tend to indicate that it might not have been murder. The suicide or accident theories don't wash either. On the other hand, according to Cynthia, Gabrielle was afraid of heights and rarely went out onto the balcony."

"I'm not ready to concede that it was not murder just yet. The chief also seems to be of the same mind. Apparently, the FBI has some interest in Gabrielle's death as they have asked for copies of our case reports."

"There must be something more here than meets the eye. To get the feds involved usually takes an act of Congress."

"By the way, did you receive the results from the lab DNA analysis?"

"The DNA in the fluids belonged to Gabrielle. None was determined to have come from anyone else."

"At least we know she wasn't the victim of a sexual assault, and from what we can determine, there was no evidence of a burglary or a robbery gone wrong."

"Until Gabrielle's boyfriend is identified and interviewed, we would be ill-advised to write off Gabrielle's death as either a suicide or an accident."

꩜

Cynthia was both devastated and frightened. On her way home, she vacantly stared out the window of the bus as it passed the UN. *I can't afford the apartment on my own. I have to think of something and pretty fast.* It was at that moment that the idea occurred to her. *I can blackmail the bastard. After all, he will probably be running for President, and I would be protecting him by not divulging what I know about his affair with Gabrielle. He is well heeled and can afford it. Why should I always have to struggle? I'm going to school trying to improve my situation, but the odds of getting a better job are pretty slim. Not only did I lose my best friend, I also lost her share of the expenses.* The two had shared confidences and Cynthia knew almost as much about Mark as did Gabrielle. She began to hatch a plan.

꩜

Cynthia surmised she could put some feelers out and see if Mark would bite. The following evening she went to the university campus and entered the computer lab. *If he has the talent or other means to trace an email, sending it from the U ensures anonymity—I hope. Darn, wish I knew how to encrypt a message. I don't dare ask one of the geeks to do that. Sending it from a public place should be safe enough. Even if it's traced back here, I'm pretty sure the sender wouldn't be identified.* The lab was a gloomy place even when it was teaming with students. At this late hour, the room was virtually empty. The hair on Cynthia's arms rose, and her skin began to tingle. She couldn't remember ever being this frightened.

Cynthia knew Mark's email address. She had looked it up in the UN's catalog many months before at Gabrielle's request when her roommate first started dating him. As she sat before the computer mentally composing her message, she reflected. *Gabrielle seemed very happy these past few days. She actually told me that she thought Mark might be going to make a commitment. How could she have been so wrong?* Cynthia shook her head in an attempt to clear the cobwebs, so she could concentrate on her message. She typed:

I know you were seeing Gabrielle LaTana on a regular basis. I understand the police are investigating her death as a possible homicide. As far as I know, they do not know who you are, only that she was seeing someone and that someone has become a person of interest. Keeping your secret comes with a price. If you are willing to negotiate, put a personal ad in the NY Daily Clip stating, 'Uncle Ralph is critical; Aunt Mary desires that you come home.' I will look for your reply in Friday's paper. If you don't reply, you leave me no choice.

Cynthia's hands were shaking as she pushed the send key. *Now I'm a criminal, a blackmailer. He'll probably kill me if he finds out it's me.*

🦢

Mark did not have the patience or the inclination to interact with Kara on any level. *She's very skilled at wearing down her opponents, and I'm not mentally or physically up to it. After all, she's put me through seven kinds of hell over the past year or so. It was because of her that I broke up with Gabrielle, and if it weren't for the breakup, Gabrielle would still be alive.* Mark, lying on his unmade bed, heard the ping from his computer that alerted him to incoming mail. *So now the bitch has resorted to email.* He turned over and pulled the sheet up around his shoulders in an attempt to ward off whatever was coming at him. Sleep evaded him. His mind was whirling and the image of Gabrielle falling to her death refused to go away. He tossed and turned. Then in desperation, he gave up and got up.

Mark went into the kitchen and opened the refrigerator. He stood with his arm draped over the door, looking inside for some inspiration. He finally decided to pour himself a glass of cold milk. *Maybe having something other than bourbon in my system will settle me down. Wish I had some sleeping pills—I desperately need to get some rest.* He gulped the milk, poured another glass, and took it with him as he ambled to his computer. As he scanned the incoming messages, one caught his eye. It was from an unknown, and his curiosity was aroused so he opened it first. Mark involuntarily jerked as he read the email, spilling his milk. "Damn, damn and damn!" he shouted at the screen. He quickly grabbed a handful of tissues from a box on his desk and began to sponge up the liquid as it slithered down his workstation. The cold milk dripped onto his bare legs and puddled around his bare feet. In exasperation, he gave up and tossed the soggy tissues into a wastepaper basket. He struggled to his feet, went into the bathroom, and turned on the shower. Mark stood under the stream until he ran out of hot water. After drying, he headed back to the computer. *I have to face the damn mess sometime, may as well be now. Hope the spill didn't ruin my keyboard.*

Wrapped in a towel, Mark stood before the computer and reread the message. He was once again engulfed by anger, only this time it was coupled with fear. *If Kara sent this. . . .it's not unlike that vicious, vindictive slut. I remember her telling me about an incident in the fourth grade when she broke a classmate's nose. She and Marie Santa Cruz squabbled over a common love interest, Don Juan, or was it Don Le Salle. She's older now and much more resourceful and, with her backing, she's probably capable of doing almost anything.* He had lost track of time, and he looked at the computer clock. *She's probably in bed. So what!* He grabbed the phone and angrily dialed her number.

"Hello," came a weak, sleepy voice.

"Right, hello yourself! Who do you think you are?" Mark shouted into the receiver.

"What? Mark is that you? I've been trying to reach you all evening. I've been worried about you. What's going on?"

"Sure you have, worried to the point of blackmailing me."

"What are you talking about? I'm not trying to blackmail you. What would I have to blackmail you with?" Kara replied. *Could he have found out about the photographs?*

"Are you saying you didn't send me an email just now asking for money in exchange for your silence?"

"No! Silence regarding what? And I need *your* money? Get real!" Kara retorted.

"Oh, never mind. It's probably some prankster trying to weasel money out of me. Go back to sleep and we'll talk later."

"No you don't! You don't get off that easy. You don't call me in the middle of the night, accuse me of blackmail, and then poo-poo it off. What did the email say?"

"Someone thinks I may have had something to do with Gabrielle's death. I did know her, she manicured my nails from time-to-time, but that was the extent of our involvement. This is all so perplexing. If someone thinks he knows something and goes to the police suggesting I killed her, I wouldn't have a leg to stand on. I do have an alibi. I was on the train going back to DC at approximately that time of day, and I save my tickets for reimbursement purposes. But wouldn't you know it? I can't find that damn ticket. I've looked in every pocket in my closet. I think I may have pulled it out with some bills when I paid for my drink downstairs after I returned home and left it setting on the bar. Joe is so efficient he probably swooped it up with his bar towel and threw it in the trash. God knows where it is now. Even if I could prove my innocence, my political career is over."

"Take it easy Mark. Anyone can say anything. Just by saying it, doesn't make it so. If this person is shooting from the hip and can't back it up with any evidence, why are you so worried?"

"Wouldn't you be a little bit concerned if someone was blackmailing you? Come on, Kara, 'what am I so concerned about'? I've got a good shot, make that a great shot, at the White House, and I don't want gossip and innuendoes spoiling my chances. I'm considering paying the demand just to get the whole thing behind me."

"Why would you do that if you're innocent? Think about it, Mark. Do you really think this is a one-time demand? Whoever it is will probably keep coming back until the well runs dry."

"I'm not so sure."

"You're not thinking right. Don't be a fool. No one who would make that kind of demand, especially of a Presidential candidate, would be satisfied with a token pay off."

"Okay, then what do you suggest?"

"I suggest we sleep on it and revisit the issue tomorrow when we're both fresh. I want to help you."

"You make it sound like I can just fall asleep without a worry in the world. *You* get real, like that's going to happen," Mark said. He didn't have the strength or desire to argue. "Let's table this until tomorrow. I need to come to the city on business. I'll leave early and come by your place first thing in the morning. Does that work for you?"

"Sure. I don't have to be at the embassy until ten so any time before then…"

"Okay, see you around eight-thirty. Night."

After Kara hung up, she stood staring at the phone. *What just happened? How could that be? Did someone else see Mark looking over the balcony? Could Simson have emailed Mark with a blackmail demand? He may be a slimy individual, but he does have some principles. He insisted that he gave me the only set of photographs. Besides, he did some work for my father and knows who he is. He'd be an idiot to poke that tiger.* Still pondering the situation, Kara slipped back into her bed and eventually fell into an exhausted dreamless sleep.

Mark spent the remainder of the night pacing up and down. *I should just pay this bastard and have it done with and let the chips fall where they may.* He wrung his hands. *Perhaps if I pay him initially, he'll let it go, at least until after the election. When I'm elected President, I'll be in a better position to provide more than money. If he's smart, he'll realize that.* The more Mark thought about it, the better he liked it. He still trusted his instincts. Upon making the decision, he went to bed and after a few agonizing minutes fell asleep.

Breakfast was ready when Mark arrived at 8:30. Kara opened the door and Mark stepped into the foyer. Kara was stunned by his appearance. He looked terrible. He had lost weight and his clothes no longer fit; dark circles underscored puffy bloodshot eyes. He looked like he hadn't shaved in a week. He needed a haircut and his hands were shaking. Walking past her, he gave a quick peck on her cheek and proceeded into the kitchen. She noticed his breath was foul, his shirt was wrinkled, and his socks didn't match. She followed, helping him out of his suit coat and draped it over a chair.

"H-m-m-m, something smells good," Mark said as he slumped onto a barstool. "I don't remember if I ate yesterday." He shook out a napkin and placed it on his lap. Kara never took her eyes off him as she set a plate before him and took the seat across from him. She toyed with a piece of toast as she watched Mark attack the bacon and eggs. He never looked up as he ravenously devoured the food. Once his hunger was satisfied, he leaned back holding a fresh cup of coffee that Kara had poured.

"You're a life saver. That breakfast was the best thing that's happened to me all week. Thank you for the hospitality and sticking with me through this nightmare."

"It is the least I can do. Even though I'm upset with you, I still care about you." Kara cleared away the dishes. "Geez, you look like the walking dead."

"I haven't been eating or sleeping, and it's beginning to take its toll. I've considered all my options and have decided to pay the blackmailer and hopefully put him at bay until after the election," Mark said as he held his cup out for a refill.

"But the election is several months off and you haven't even been nominated yet. Do you think this person is going to hibernate and wait until after the election is over before asking you for another payment?" Kara filled Mark's cup and left the room. When she came back, she handed Mark a small pink razor. "Here, take this and go shave."

"Thanks. Guess I forgot. I've been so preoccupied." He walked toward the bathroom and paused. "I don't see any alternative to this situation. If you have a better plan, let's hear it."

"I don't, but I'm afraid your plan is not very reasonable."

"At least that'll buy me some time to come up with a better idea. Do women use shaving cream?"

"It's in the medicine cabinet. Have you considered hiring a private investigator? Maybe you should try to find out the identity of the blackmailer." Kara slouched against the doorjamb and watched Mark shave with the tiny razor. His face looked pale and drawn under the bright lights positioned over the bathroom mirror.

"I want to keep this as close to the vest as possible," Mark replied. "Ouch! How do you ever get something the size of your legs shaved with this toy?"

"What do you mean 'the size of my legs'?" Kara asked as she gave Mark a disapproving glance.

"Oh, for Pete's sake. I meant in comparison to my face. Your legs are not big. They're perfect and I should know. I've seen them up close and personal," Mark said, forcing a smile.

"Nice save, Mark," Kara said. "Investigators can be very discreet. I happen to know one that my dad used several years ago. Do you want me to contact him for you?"

"Are you serious? Do you really think an investigator can track down this creep? Ouch, damn it!"

"Yes, in fact, I do. Sit down and let me help you. Otherwise your face is going to look like raw hamburger," Kara coaxed as she took the razor from him and motioned him toward the toilet seat.

Mark complied. "If hiring an investigator is going to cost as much as making the blackmail payment, then what do I gain if your man can't come up with a name?"

"He is very reasonable. In fact, he owes me a favor and I believe he'll do this as repayment of the favor." Kara finished shaving Mark.

"You know I can't use any of my donations to pay a private investigator. If that got out, my goose would be cooked. However, you have piqued my interest. Call him and see what he thinks but don't mention my name," Mark said, splashing water on his face. He grabbed a towel and dabbed at his skin.

Kara pointed to the mouthwash. Mark took the hint and rinsed his mouth.

"I have to run now, but I'll come by this evening before I catch the train back to DC. Thanks for breakfast and the shave."

"Try to relax, Mark. You're much too tense. People will notice. I should have some information for you by this evening."

"I don't know how I can relax with so much going on in my life right now. See you tonight." He gave Kara another quick peck on the cheek and left. He couldn't decide if he was relieved or not. His head was spinning with the crisis in which he found himself, and he was unable to see any light at the end of the tunnel.

⟡

As soon as Mark left, Kara called Vern Simson.

"Yeah, Simson here."

"Vern. It's Kara Isabella, do you have a minute?"

"Yes, ma'am," Vern answered in a singsong manner.

Kara went on to explain the situation to Simson using names since Simson was already in the know. Listening, Simson sat up straighter. He was extremely interested in taking on the case. It was the type of investigation he relished back in his years on the police force in the Special Crimes Unit. As soon as Simson heard about the blackmail plot, he was curious—curious enough to want to enter the fray. Besides, he was already a part of it.

"Money seems to be a consideration. How much would you charge?"

"Same as I charged you before, fifteen thousand plus expenses. There's no guessing how much the expenses will amount to. You just have to take your chances. Of course, my fee comes with a vow of silence. Take it or leave it."

"I have to run it by Mark but I'm thinking he'll take it. I'll let you know tomorrow. How soon can you start?"

"As soon as I'm provided the fifteen grand," Vern answered, "I'll make the assignment a priority for a friend of a former client."

"I know Mark will appreciate that," Kara said.

Early that evening a very bedraggled Mark rang Kara's doorbell. He was extremely pale and looked even worse than he had that morning.

"You better come in and sit down," Kara urged, taking Mark's arm and leading him to his favorite leather recliner. He dropped into it and leaned forward cupping his face in his hands.

Kara looked at him for a moment with an amalgam of contempt and pity. "I'll get you a drink. Looks like you had a rough day."

"This whole charade is wearing me down," Mark said dejectedly. "Did you line up the investigator?"

"Yes, I did," she replied, handing him a glass of scotch.

Mark sipped the drink and leaned back against the leather chair.

"He agreed to take the case because he owes me a favor, and we agreed that his fee would be the repayment of that favor," Kara said as she gulped deeply from her own glass, feeling the warmth of the alcohol in her throat and the tang of her deception. She never took her eyes off Mark. "That's quite an offer if you ask me."

Mark nodded as he took another sip from his glass.

"He will need a copy of the email before he can get started. If you want, send it to me and I will forward it to him," Kara offered, hoping Mark would take the bait.

"Thanks, but I would rather deal personally with the investigator. I do appreciate everything you've done, but it's my problem and I need to be in the eye of the storm." Mark took another sip from his drink while squinting at Kara.

"Suit yourself. Just trying to be helpful." Kara got up and poured herself another drink. "Need a refill?" she asked.

"No thanks," Mark said as he drained his glass. "Don't think I'm not grateful for all you've done. You've been very helpful, and I can never repay you but you've done enough. I need to deal with whatever comes down the pike myself and in my own way. Give me the investigator's name and number."

"Of course." Kara walked to her desk to write down the information. *How am I going to juggle this?* She had a thought just then. "Mark, it would be better if I had him call you. Since he doesn't know who you are because I didn't mention names at your request, he may not take the call. I'll call him first thing in the morning and give him your phone number."

"That makes sense," Mark mumbled. "I should go if I'm going to catch the 8:30 back to DC."

Walking him to the door, Kara looked up with what she hoped was a reassuring smile. Mark gave her the traditional good-bye peck as he left.

As soon as Mark was gone, Kara telephoned Vern. She told him what had transpired and gave him Mark's telephone number. Vern asked about payment. An exasperated Kara told him she would meet him at the usual location the next day at noon and bring the cash. Kara had decided she would pay Vern knowing Mark had put all of his savings into his campaign. She was anxious to find out who the blackmailer was.

"Works for me. See ya then," Simson responded.

Kara's reserve had been exhausted so she called her father and asked him to wire $100,000 to her bank account. Giovanni Isabella didn't even blink an eye.

"My, my. What's my little girl been buying that's so expensive?"

"Oh, you know Daddy. It costs a lot to live in New York, and I have to keep up appearances. The future First Lady can't wear clothing off the rack. You trained me better than that."

"That's my girl. I'll get the transfer to you as soon as the bank opens. How's the campaign going?"

"Polls show Mark has an edge on the competition, thanks to you and your support. Give my love to Mother." Kara was eager to end the call— she had much to do.

"How 'bout me?"

"Oh, Daddy, that goes without saying. Of course, I love you best."

"That's what I wanted to hear. Keep in touch. I love you, too."

"Bye now."

Kara hung up the phone. *This is costing a fortune but it's worth it. How do you put a price on revenge?*

Who in the hell could be blackmailing Mark and with what? I have all of the photographs. That is, if I can believe Vern Simson.

When Mark returned home from the office, he had a message from Simson asking him to return his call. Mark had been anxious the entire day and was ready to get some results, so he immediately telephoned Vern.

"Mr. Simson, this is Senator Mark Langford. I understand Kara Isabella explained to you my predicament. I cannot even fathom what anyone would have to use to blackmail me. I'm hoping you can get to the bottom of this."

"If anyone can, it would be me. That's not a brag—I just simply am the best. I need a copy of the email for starters."

"What is your email address? I'll send it to you as soon as we hang up. You have my phone number and will now have my email address. I would appreciate a daily update."

"Whoa, a daily update may be asking a lot. Matters of this nature take technical manipulation, and I may not have daily results. I will, however, keep you posted regarding my progress."

"Okay," Mark hesitated, "Obviously, I don't know how these things work. I just want to have this nightmare behind me."

"I'll be in touch."

Before drifting off that night, Mark thought, *At least I'm doing something that really beats the hell out of doing nothing. For the first time in a* week, Mark fell into a restful, undisturbed sleep. He liked Simson's confidence. It was reassuring.

*   *   *

The following morning Kara contacted Vern to find out what transpired between Mark and him. She was still miffed that Mark wouldn't forward the email to her and curiosity was getting the better of her. "Vern, its Kara. How did it go with Mark?"

"Just fine." The seasoned veteran knew a lead-in when he heard it.

Kara was beyond impatient and resented Simson's games. "What did the email say?"

"Now, you know I can't reveal anything that's confidential to an investigation."

"Damn you! I'm paying you, you're working for me," Kara slammed her fist down on the desk.

"H-m-m-m, that's not what I understood. Langford said *he* agreed to my terms. I'm under the impression I'm working for him no matter where the payment comes from, and he didn't say you were personally paying my fees."

Kara was cornered. She didn't respond.

"Still there?" Vern quarried.

"Yes."

"Do we meet or do I just drop the case and get on with life?"

"We meet," a very dejected Kara responded.

"Well, all righty then. I'll see you the same time, at the same place. Cash only, remember?"

Once again, Kara's phone went flying across the room, smashing against the wall. Not willing to give it up altogether, her last hope was with a face-to-face confrontation. *Maybe I can con Vern into telling me something. What do I have to lose? Now all I have to do is get the money and get it to Vern. Damn those bastards! Not only am I kept in the dark, I have to pay for the privilege.*

Vern was sitting at a table outside the diner, thumbing through a magazine and drinking a soda, when Kara arrived. That *déjà vu* feeling slid across her mind as she sat down and stared at him. He did not immediately look up. The fact that he would openly display so much disrespect infuriated her. She slammed the bag of money down on the table making him jump and look up. "Oh, it's you. 'Bout time you got here. I thought you may have changed your mind."

"Oh, come on, Vern. I'm not that late. It took more time than I planned getting the money together but it's all here," Kara said still holding onto the bag as Vern reached for it. "Not so fast. I think I'm entitled to some information in exchange for such a large amount of cash. All I want to know is what the email said."

"And I'm still telling you I can't reveal any information. It would be unethical on my part. I can't risk my reputation. However, if it's any comfort, you can rest in the knowledge that all of our transactions are just as confidential."

Kara bit back her anger. The last thing she needed was to alienate Vern. "Okay, that makes sense. I guess I just want to know what I'm paying for."

"I understand where you're coming from, but unfortunately, I can't compromise my ethics."

Kara released her grip on the money bag and slid it across the table to Vern. Vern took the bag, scanned its contents and rose from his chair, "You might think about putting me on retainer. It's cheaper that way."

Kara ignored the remark. She sensed Vern was abrasive by nature and treated everyone with distain. As he turned and walked away, she could not help but wonder about what sinister plot he might have up his sleeve. His brashness must have a purpose.

Simson had an acquaintance that possessed unbelievable computer skills. In fact, she was so good she was nicknamed Dotcom. Simson didn't know her by any other name and had never met her in person. He always contacted her via email. Upon receiving the payment from Kara, Simson went to his apartment and forwarded Dot the blackmail email.

Good afternoon, Dot. I've attached an email. I need to know where it originated. I will deposit your fee in the usual manner by placing $500 in an envelope and putting it in your mail drop.

Dot emailed back her willingness to oblige and her agreement to the $500 fee. It didn't take her very long to trace the source of the email to the NYU computer lab. She emailed her findings to Simson.

The original source is a computer lab at NYU. I don't see how that can be helpful in light of so many potential users, but at least, we narrowed it down. Hopefully, it will provide a lead.

BINGO! Simson knew Gabrielle LaTana's roommate attended the U. The connection was not even supposition. It all made sense but what would he do with the knowledge? He did have some scruples. *If Mark had pushed Gabrielle off the balcony, what would stop him from killing her roommate to ensure her silence? And then what would stop him from killing me to guarantee my silence? Since he's being groomed for a run at the White House, how far would he go to protect his reputation? I'm pretty sure I know the answer, and Langford probably has the resources at his disposal to get the job done. After all, who wouldn't want the President beholding to them. H-m-m-m, interesting equation. I better sleep on it.* And so he did.

CHAPTER 9

DEVIL AND THE DEEP BLUE SEA

SIMSON HAD THE CASH and he had made no guarantee to either Mark or Kara that he would be able to find out who had sent the blackmail demand. Although he bragged to Mark that he was the best, the fact remained that he was. He knew who had sent the email, but he was not willing to share that with Mark, at least not at the present time. He decided to have a conversation with Cynthia and confirm her role in the blackmail scam. So, to that end, the next day he called the number corresponding with the address from his previous surveillance of Mark by using the reverse telephone directory.

"Hello," Cynthia answered in a weak, almost frightened voice.

"Cynthia?"

"Yes."

"I'm a friend of a friend and I want to meet with you. I think you know what it's about."

Cynthia's quick intake of breath startled Vern, but confirmed his suspicion that she had sent the email. "You have nothing to fear from me," he said. "I truly mean you no harm. However, there are others who are not so trusting and pose a threat. I suggest you hear what I have to say for your own good."

Cynthia was trapped. Someone traced the email. "How do I know you can be trusted?"

"You'll just have to risk that. We can meet in a public place where there are lots of people. You pick the venue."

After a slight hesitation, Cynthia said, "The library at the university at 3:00 p.m. this afternoon?"

"That works. I'll be easy to spot as I'll be sitting close to the rear exit reading Carroll Multz' latest novel, *The Chameleon*." Vern had previously read all six of Multz' mystery/courtroom novels but especially liked *The Chameleon*. Vern could relate to the protagonist, an undercover cop dubbed the great imposter, who out-conned the cons—pretty much like himself.

"When you get there, if you don't like the looks of things and since I don't know what you look like, you can just walk back out and forget we ever talked."

"Okay, I can agree to that," Cynthia said, her voice quivering.

"Cynthia, no harm will come to you from meeting with me. That's a guarantee."

"Why should I trust you?" Cynthia asked once again.

"You have no reason to. But why would I go to all of this trouble if I meant to harm you?"

"Okay, point made. I. . .I'll be there," she said.

ॐ

The parking lots nearest the NYU library were full when Vern arrived and he was forced to park

in a handicap slot. He was confident he wouldn't
be towed because of his contrived handicapped
placard. Vern was familiar with the library, as
he had used it for research on several occasions.
He arrived early and took up a position where
he could see the only entrance to the library.
After a few minutes, a very nervous young lady
appeared. She continually looked over her shoulder as she tentatively entered the main doors.
Vern surmised it was Cynthia, because of her
furtive movements and he felt sorry for her. *Poor
little thing, she was really out of her element with
the blackmail gig.*

Cynthia apparently didn't see Vern as she
seated herself at a table closest to the rear facing the entry. Well, so much for planning ahead,
Vern thought as he slipped *The Chameleon* into his
jacket pocket. Vern approached her table and took
a seat across from her. Cynthia jumped when he
sat down. Vern had mimicked a professor and wore
navy blue slacks, white button-down shirt, paisley
tie, and camel sports jacket. He had smoothed his
hair back and taken on an intellectual air.

"Try not to look so scared," he said in what he
hoped was a comforting tone, "I'm not here to
harm you."

"What is it you want?"

"Basically, to save your life."

Once again, the sudden intake of air. "Why?
Do you think I'm in danger?"

"I was hired by Mark Langford to find out
who sent him the extortion email. It didn't take
a genius to figure it out. He doesn't know what I

know, and I'm not going to tell him if you do what I tell you."

Cynthia sat there squinting. Her eyes narrowed as she examined Vern's stern expression.

"Cynthia, you are in danger. If I don't get back to my client with answers, he will hire someone else. I have a plan to throw him off for a while, but you have to disappear."

"How can I? I don't umm—"

"I know. I'm prepared to make you an offer. In this envelope," Vern said, holding up a manila envelope, "I have the money Langford paid me to find you. If you promise me you will disappear, I will give you the $15,000 to make a new start somewhere far, far from here."

"And just why would you do that?"

Vern perceived that Cynthia's suspicions were on overload. "Because I'm a nice guy, and you remind me of my sister. That's all you need to know. Do we have a deal?"

"Yes!" Cynthia all but shouted.

"Okay then. I'd like to suggest that you just leave. Tell no one, and I do mean no one, where you're going. Pack your personal belongings and just go. It's important that you cover your tracks. Langford has deep pockets and long arms if you catch my drift." He observed that she was absorbing what he was telling her. Cynthia carefully picked up the envelope and put it in her backpack.

"Thank you, whoever you are. I was never comfortable being a criminal anyway. God bless you and I promise I will go as far from this place as possible."

"Good decision. I'll send up a smoke screen, which will give you at least a week. Don't bother to drop classes and don't let your landlord know you're leaving. Don't divulge your plan to anyone, not even your best friend. I hope you're taking this seriously as your very life depends on it."

"No worries there. I can hardly wait to get away from here. Do you think he killed her?"

"Don't know for sure, but why take the chance. Right now, you're between the devil and the deep blue sea. Get going and good luck."

Cynthia stood and shouldered her backpack. She slipped past the back of Vern's chair, leaned over, and planted a gentle kiss on the top of his head. Then she was gone. Stunned, Vern sat for a few minutes. That had never happened to him, and before he returned to the real world, he wanted to bask in the euphoric sensation of being spontaneously kissed by a foxy lady.

On the drive back to his office, Vern thought back to the Kennedy assignation and how many people had to die to divert the finger of guilt. Vern knew Cynthia's survival was the key to his survival.

Kara was out of options, there was nowhere to go. Mark and Vern, the only two people who had the information she wanted, weren't talking. She had festered with rage all day and lay exhausted on her bed. She couldn't even think of a Plan B. Poor little rich girl, she never went down with dignity. As she lay on the verge of sleep, she promised herself, *I'll get even with 'em. Both of 'em.* That thought appeased her as she drifted off.

Vern waited until the next day to contact Mark. Mark's assistants were efficient and screened his calls carefully.

"Look, Honey, the Senator is waiting for this call. I wouldn't want to be in your shoes when he finds out you didn't put me through."

A scant ten seconds passed before Vern heard Langford's voice, "Yes, what is so important?"

"This is Simson. So far, no luck. But I believe I told you this would take time. Have you heard back from the perp?"

"Oh, Mr. Simson. I didn't know it was you. My receptionist got your name wrong. No, I have had no more contacts since the initial email. What do you think will happen if I don't get the ad in the paper as I was instructed?"

"I don't think the blackmailer will give up that easily. If the ad doesn't appear, I suspect he'll give it another try. If the extortionist has anything worth selling, he isn't going to waste it without exhausting all his resources. This scheme has all the earmarks of an amateur, and if you capitulate, he won't let you off the hook. Easy money is easy money. You, of course, have the option of placing the ad and seeing what happens. Your decision."

"If I decide to place the ad, I need to get it in today to make the deadline. You're the expert. What do you suggest?" There was worry in Mark's voice.

"Hold off. The blackmailer isn't going to give up without a fight. If he does what he threatened to do, he will have in essence killed the goose. I have a few more cards up my sleeve, but I need more time."

"Okay. Since I'm paying you for your expertise, I'll take your advice but God help you if you're wrong."

"Whoa, that sounds like a threat. I never promised you anything, and I take exception to being talked to like that. If you're having second thoughts, I will be more than happy to return your money. . . ."

"No, no, don't do that! That was a knee-jerk reaction and frustration on my part. Please continue with the investigation."

"Okay, but watch what you say to me. Senator or not, I won't tolerate being threatened and pushed around."

"I understand. How soon do you think you will have something to report?"

"A few days at most. I'll call you when I know something worth reporting. Remember these things take time." Vern closed his cell phone and ended the call.

As Vern slid his phone into his jacket pocket, he kicked back and put his feet on his desk. He retrieved the bourbon from the bottom desk drawer and poured himself three fingers. Then he took a cigar out of the humidor, his favorite brand, *La Traviata*, and examined it as though it were a beautiful woman just waiting to be enjoyed. He finally lit it and held his glass in one hand and the cigar in the other. He reared back and, looking up at the ceiling, filled the air with smoke rings. He had bought Cynthia at least a week, and he felt good about that.

⚶

Mark was too distraught at first to register the disrespectful way Vern hung up. His future was hanging by a thread, and he put his life in the hands of someone he believed to be of disreputable character. *Damn Kara anyway. How is it she knows this reprobate?* He slammed down his receiver.

⚶

Cynthia was apprehensive about venturing out on her own. There had always been someone to lean on. With Gabrielle gone, she had no one. Even the advice from a stranger was more than she had yesterday, and something she held on to. She had no recourse but to follow Vern's advice. Survival dictated she follow through on her self-imposed exile.

Cynthia opened the door of the apartment. *At least I won't have to live here any longer. The cops can pound sand. I just do not trust them. They made a mess of the apartment and left it for me to clean up. Starting over somewhere else is beginning to have more-and-more appeal. Where will I go? I could stay with Aunt Margaret in Virginia. But would I be bringing my troubles to her doorstep? I can't take that chance; Aunt Margaret is in her seventies and doesn't need any trauma at this stage of life. Okay then, having a choice of going anywhere on this planet, where would I go?* Then it hit her. *New Orleans! Yes, New Orleans. One of the best times I've ever had was spent in New Orleans.* Thus, the decision was made. Cynthia began packing with a renewed spirit. She had decided upon a destination.

Emptying the desk she shared with her late roommate, she found Gabrielle's green card. Twisting the card between her fingers, it occurred to her. *I can use Gabrielle's ID, and if I paid for my ticket in cash, there would not be an obvious trail for anyone to follow. I look enough like Gabrielle that if anyone looked closely at the picture on the card, I could pull it off. Gabrielle was fifteen pounds lighter and a couple of inches shorter but who bothers to check that.* She interrupted her packing to call a travel agent and reserve a ticket to New Orleans. The sooner the better, she thought. Two and a half hours later, Cynthia boarded a flight with a group of party-goers celebrating the anniversary of two of their friends.

CHAPTER 10

Beauty is Only Skin Deep

IT WAS ONLY TWO WEEKS before that Monacan Ambassador Omar Paulin learned of his sister's death. Gabrielle was his only sibling. Grief stricken, he took her body home to Monaco to be buried alongside their parents, Michelle and Tomas. The weekend he returned to New York after Gabrielle's funeral, Omar, wanting to catch up on his work, took a cab to his office. No matter how he tried, he was unable to concentrate on the tasks at hand. He was hounded by the tragic death of his sister and the fragile nature of life. He reflected on the series of events that brought him to this time and place.

Omar graduated from the University of Monte Carlo and was immediately employed by the government as assistant to the financial director. He had been in that position for three years when he was promoted as aid to the Monarch. His language, financial and social skills had not gone unnoticed, so when Joseph Cortes, the ambassador to the UN, died suddenly of a heart attack, Omar was asked by Monarch Francisco to temporarily fill the position. Although Omar possessed all of the skills necessary to be an effective ambassador, protocol dictated that other candidates also be considered.

"Omar, your loyalty, education, and language skills are credentials enough to entitle you to a permanent appointment, but we must follow the rules. It will take several months to wade through, weed out and interview those applicants who appear to be most qualified. We are calling your appointment temporary, but unless someone has better qualifications than you. . . ."

So it was settled. Omar left for New York on short notice. Ambassadors were allowed to select their embassy staff. Omar chose to retain the secretarial support staff that was already in place. But, because of the prevalence of terrorist attacks worldwide, he elected to bring his life-long friend and confident, Louis La Mar, with him. Louis would serve as a bodyguard as well as chauffer.

"Mr. Ambassador," Louis suggested, "you would be wise to include Hercules 'Herc' Valapando, whose strength and muscle emulates his namesake. I'd also suggest Mick O'Sullivan, our longtime acquaintance and electronic/computer expert, and Joseph Lancaster, whose locksmith/ safecracking skills are unequaled. You never know when you're going to need a safe cracked."

Omar looked out the bank of windows that formed one wall of his office and noticed it was already twilight. He turned back, and resting his elbows on his desk, put his head in his hands as he wept for his dead sister. Omar was grief stricken and guilt ridden over Gabrielle's death. Painfully, he remembered that fifteen years before, his parents died in a tragic accident. Their vehicle was run off the cliffs surrounding the Mediterranean during a violent rainstorm as they were returning home from a night of gambling in Monte Carlo. Although it was listed as an accident by the authorities, Omar heard rumors that Antonio Sebastian, a disgruntled customer at the bank where Omar's father was president, deliberately ran his parents' vehicle over the cliff. His suspicions were confirmed at his parents' funerals when Omar overheard bank employees whisper that Sebastian threatened his father when the bank denied Sebastian's loan application.

Reflecting back to the time his parents were killed, Omar remembered when their maternal grandmother, Camille LaTana, came to live with them. The Paulins left an adequate estate, so Camille and the children lived comfortably. Omar was seventeen and Gabrielle seven at the time their parents were killed. Upon losing her mother, Gabrielle clung to Camille. She even gave her grandmother a pet name, *Mamasetta*. Camille told Omar that she interpreted it to be Gabrielle's special version of grandmother.

Omar's employment demanded that he work out of the palace in Monte Carlo. The distance between his family home in La Condamine and Monte Carlo was too far to drive each day, so Omar moved to Monte Carlo. Despite the distance, he frequently visited his sister and grandmother.

More tears formed as he thought of the year after Gabrielle graduated high school. During one of his visits, Gabrielle announced, "I'm going to enter the upcoming Miss Monaco beauty pageant in Monte Carlo in July. The winner receives ten thousand dollars and will represent Monaco in the New World Beauty Pageant competition in Miami in the spring."

Omar painfully remembered how stunned Gabrielle was by his reaction. He had frowned and rebuked her. "Beauty pageants are trite and demeaning," he replied. "You would tarnish the family name by just entering the contest!"

The hurt and astonished expression on Gabrielle's face was burned into his memory. He relived her angry and harsh response. "That's selfish and unwarranted. You impose double standards. You're free to do as you want, but I can't? How fair is that?" She had interrupted him when he attempted to explain. "This is something I've dreamt about since I was a little girl. Who are you to dictate to me what I can and cannot do? And, just because you're so worried I'm going to slander your stellar reputation, I'll legally change my name."

At that time, Omar knew Gabrielle meant what she said. From her stubborn and unyielding past, he knew she was resolute in not only entering the pageant but also emerging with the crown.

He also remembered his final plea. "You sound like your mind's made up, and I suppose there's nothing I can say to sway you. I only wish you would reconsider."

"How do you conclude that beauty pageants are trite and demeaning? And if I win, how would that tarnish the family name? You should commend me, not condemn me."

As Gabrielle stood her ground, Omar realized that no amount of coaxing on his part would convince his sister otherwise.

Omar agonized as he remembered that was the last time he saw Gabrielle alive. Suspended between daylight and twilight, Omar recalled how difficult the trip was when he took Gabrielle's body home. Their grandmother had met him at the airport and, with Louis' help and support, transported his sister's coffin to La Condamine where Gabrielle's body was buried next to their parents.

After the funeral, his grandmother requested a private conversation with him. He was troubled as he watched her twist a tissue to shreds in nervous anticipation. She finally confided that she had overheard his argument over Gabrielle's entering the beauty pageant. She appeared to be guilt-ridden as she related her story. In his mind, he replayed the conversation verbatim. He would never forget the anxiety and sorrow his grandmother displayed as she spoke.

"That same afternoon, Omar, after you left to return to Monte Carlo, I sat down on the edge of Gabrielle's bed, and took both of her hands in mine. I revealed to her that when I was in my last year of high school, I wanted to enter a beauty pageant. I told her my father, your great grandfather, Leopold, had forbidden me from doing so.

Out of respect for him, I opted not to participate. I told Gabrielle that I had spent the better part of my life wondering how different things would have been had I had been allowed to enter. Even if I hadn't won, just entering the contest would have been a dream come true. I didn't want your sister to follow suit and live the rest of her life in regret. I told her that I supported her decision and encouraged her to follow her dream and not let opportunities slip through her fingers like so many grains of sand.

"I also told her that since you had a high-profile position with the government, I respected your reluctance about using the family name. It was then I suggested she use my last name, LaTana, your mother's maiden name, when she entered the pageant. By doing so we could alleviate your concern and at the same time, Gabrielle could pursue her dream."

Omar recalled his grandmother relating her experience. "I saw the anguish melt from Gabrielle's face and she fell into my arms and sobbed. She finally managed to say, 'Oh, Mamasetta, thank you, thank you, thank you. I'd be honored to use your name.' Then she did the most amazing thing. She went to her jewelry box and brought out a small gold cross. I remembered your mother had presented it to her when she made her confirmation at Our Lady of Sorrows. Gabrielle fastened the cross around my neck." His grandmother lovingly touched the cross as she continued her story. "I've worn it ever since. I never remove it. It's part of my daughter and my granddaughter. I loved them so much, and they both died a tragic death." At that point, he could barely hear her as she sobbed. "Perhaps if I hadn't encouraged her to follow her dream, she would still be alive. It's my fault, it's my fault. *Mea culpa, mea culpa, mea maxima culpa.*"

Omar reflected on that day as he listened to his grandmother's confession barely a week before. His heart went out to her. When she broke down, he took her in his arms, trying to console her. Then he, too, had been overcome with emotion.

"Oh, Grandmother, like you, I'm haunted with guilt and grief. If I'd only been more understanding and compassionate. . . Gabrielle and I both lived in New York, but we never saw each other. We both harbored hard feelings, and I remember being resentful at what I considered her calloused attitude and stubbornness. I'm ashamed of my conduct, and I pray daily for forgiveness from both the Lord and Gabrielle."

Omar's reverie was interrupted when the red phone on his desk rang. Only a few individuals had the number to his private line, so he picked it up immediately.

"This is Ambassador Paulin."

"Omar, I've been searching all over for you," Louis said. Omar detected the relief in Louis' voice.

"Sorry, my friend. I came to the office to catch up and lost track of time. Can you join me at my residence for dinner? I want to run something by you."

"Of course. If you're ready to leave, I'll pick you up. How did you get there anyway?"

"Since it is your day off, I took a taxi."

"Omar, I don't take days off. I'm not just another employee. You're taking your life in your hands when you ride with a cabbie."

Omar laughed. "I'm ready to leave. Where are you?"

"Not far from there. Be there in ten."

Both men were silent on the drive to the Monacan residence. After dinner, Omar suggested they retire to his study.

"I could use a brandy, how 'bout you?"

"Sure, let me pour." Louis headed for the bar.

"Louis, I'm not convinced Gabrielle committed suicide. It's been haunting me and I'd like for us to conduct our own investigation. The locals are doing what they can, but they don't have the fire in their belly to really dig."

"Great minds. I was thinking the same thing. Gabe was like a sister to me."

"Yes, I know. You've been like a brother to us both since our school days," Omar said, squeezing Louis' shoulder. "Now my thoughts. Since you're the expert, I'm seeking your sage advice. We don't have many clues to hang our hats on. Gabrielle and I never communicated with each other although we were both living here in New York. I sent her roses and congratulated her on winning Miss Monaco but she didn't acknowledge either one. I think that silly disagreement really affected her, and she chose to cut me off from her life almost completely. She mentioned in a letter to Grandmother LaTana that she was seeing a Senator by the name of Mark. She didn't give a last name or, for that matter, any other information. Your suggestion that we bring your three cronies along was a stroke of genius. They will come in handy if you agree to my plan."

"I have a confession to make. When I suggested we bring Herc, Mick, and Joseph, I had ulterior motives. We've been poking around, and I have some information concerning the Senator."

"Un huh! Holding out on me?"

"Nope, just gathering information. That's why I was trying to locate you today. Not knowing how you would react, I wanted something solid before we talked. I finally got the break I was looking for. Just today, I talked to Mick who has been dating a girl who worked with Gabe at *BellaDonna*. Lacy, Mick's girl, told him she thought the Senator was Mark Langford, the Senator from Indiana. She reasoned that Gabe manicured Langford's nails bimonthly, and it seemed to her to be more than a business relationship. I did some follow up and determined that Langford is also courting the interpreter from the Spanish Embassy, a fox by the name of Kara Isabella."

"So, we have a place to start. I've been in meetings with Ambassador Madrid and have seen Isabella. She's quite the looker. You and your crew keep digging; I'm going to follow up on the Isabella lead."

"Oh, sure, I have to work with Dopey, Sleepy and Grumpy and you get Snow White.

How fair is that?"

"Rank has its privileges."

CHAPTER 11

FLIRTING WITH DISASTER

AMBASSADOR MADRID was hosting a luncheon at the UN for ambassadors from Portugal, Monaco, Italy, and France. The Delegates Dining Room was bordered by the colorful flags of the UN's 191 member states and provided an impressive backdrop for corporate and/or social functions. Designed to fascinate viewers both day and night, the floor-to-ceiling windows with 180-degree views overlooked the East River and New York City's majestic skyline. It was said that "Guests will feel inspired in this world renowned setting where diplomats, ambassadors and world leaders dine, celebrate and arbitrate."

Kara was fluent in each of the languages of the five attendee states and was looking forward to an afternoon in the world-renowned dining room, mingling with interesting and influential people. There was almost always a gentleman or two who took an interest in her. However, during the time she was with Mark and particularly after they became engaged, she put her heart on a shelf believing that she and Mark were destined to be together.

A few days before the luncheon, Kara purchased a stunning dress. She had brought the gown in a garment bag to work that morning and

made the change just before the festivities began
to avoid getting it wrinkled or otherwise mussed.
She stood before the mirrors in the private ladies'
room adjacent to the Spanish suite of offices and
surveyed herself. *Yes, this dress is a lulu.* It showed
off her figure to every advantage without actually
revealing a single thing.

The ambassador was also ready, so when she
entered his office, he came around his desk and
extended his arm. Kara looped hers through his,
and he escorted her to the dining room.

When the two of them entered, conversation
stopped and all eyes turned in their direction. As
they wove their way through the seated guests
and approached the head table, Kara, walked a
few steps behind the ambassador, watching carefully as he nodded greetings and shook hands. She
was always ready to interpret if she sensed he did
not comprehend what was being said. She was in
essence his Girl Friday, and she knew her value
but did not take advantage of it. Oddly enough,
that was the one part of her life she didn't manip-
ulate. Kara truly loved her job and would therefore
do nothing to jeopardize it. She was paid well but,
of course, financially she didn't need a salary, so
that wasn't a consideration as far as her career was
concerned.

Kara sensed the attention she drew as they
slowly moved across the dining room. She, not the
ambassador, was the center of attention and she
played her role to the hilt. She walked a little more
seductively and held her head slightly higher than
usual. When she bent to listen to a conversation,

she placed her hands on her knees and leaned forward, making sure her bosom, enhanced by a black lace pushup bra, showed just a little from the scooped neck of the jade silk dress. *That should make their thighs tingle.* Straightening, she playfully brushed a few tendrils of hair over her shoulder and slightly shook her head, rearranging her long hair and pretending not to notice the male attention she drew. Because it was expected, she focused her attention on the ambassador.

Kara was always seated at the ambassador's left, which was another perk that came with the position. When they finally took their places at the head table, Ambassador Madrid stood and welcomed his guests. The luncheon was intended to be relaxed, so the delegates could get to know one another. The atmosphere was intentionally light and casual. Ambassador Madrid took a sip of water and placed his napkin in his lap. He smiled and looked around and then bowed his head in silent thanks to his Christian God. When he looked up, he nodded and the wait staff began serving.

⤳

By his glances, Omar made it readily apparent that he had more than a casual interest in Kara. He was seated two positions from her, so he boldly approached the guest seated next to Kara, the interpreter for the Portuguese ambassador, and politely asked if he would mind changing places. By moving, the Portuguese interpreter would be repositioned on the other side of his ambassador, so the move was not disruptive. The guest graciously agreed and immediately rose to give Ambassador Paulin his place. Before Paulin sat down, he bowed to Kara and introduced himself. Kara was absorbed in the conversation between Ambassador Madrid and French Ambassador Maurice Dupree, so when Omar Paulin addressed her, she appeared surprised. As he spoke her name, she turned and looked up. He smiled down at her.

Kara's first thought was his photograph does not do him justice. She recognized the ambassador from Monaco from a photograph in his dossier. Kara was required to read the dossiers of the guests prior to attending functions. Ambassador Madrid depended on her knowledge to help him knowingly converse with other guests. Recovering somewhat from her surprise, she gestured to the empty chair and offered him her hand as she said, "I am so happy to make your acquaintance, Ambassador Paulin."

"And I yours," Omar replied as he gently placed a kiss on the back of Kara's hand. "I trust you do not think it too bold of me to have changed places in order to sit by you. If you were me and your choice was to be sandwiched between two boring men or next to an intriguing woman, which would you pick?"

"If you were me, you'd be pleased with the selection. It's not often I get to sit next to the most handsome man in the room."

"You have discerning taste in addition to being beautiful."

Gazing into Omar's chiseled tanned face dominated by dark blazing eyes and a broad gleaming smile, Kara felt a sensation she had never felt before, not even with Mark.

For a long moment, their eyes were entangled in amazement, enchantment, and intrigue. Neither said anything until Ambassador Madrid interrupted with a greeting directed at Ambassador Paulin.

"Omar, I see you have met my interpreter. Didn't realize we were seated in such close proximity."

"You might say I invoked ambassadorial privileges in being seated next to the second most influential ambassador to the UN and the most captivating woman I've seen grace the halls of this institution."

"Watch out for him," Ambassador Madrid said to Kara. "His judgment is at issue when he doesn't rightfully recognize who is *the* most influential ambassador at the UN."

"Give me credit, Carlos. At least I was on all fours when I described your interpreter," Omar said smiling at Kara.

"Being half right does give you some credibility. However, being correct about something so obvious as with Kara and then so incorrect as putting me in second place, does call into question your ability to be correct one hundred percent of the time."

"Reasonable people might differ about who is the most influential ambassador at the UN," Omar said. "Some say it is Samantha Power, the ambassador from the United States. Others say, and rightfully so, that it is me."

"How did I get into the middle of this?" Kara asked. The three laughed and toasted to the most influential ambassador at the UN "whoever that may be."

Kara relished in the attention she received from both sides of her. The bantering between the two seemed to be for her benefit. Ambassador Madrid appeared to be unusually possessive and protective. Ambassador Paulin, on the other hand, seemed to be on something other than a goodwill mission.

Kara was impressed by Omar's command of the English language and his wit. He was dignified yet personable; intellectual yet not overbearing; and warm but not gushing.

As dessert was served, Kara found herself comfortable in Omar's presence and receptive to his suggestion that she visit the Monacan consulate.

"I'd love to," she remarked. "What is the best time for you?"

"How about tomorrow?" Omar asked.

"But it's a Saturday. Wouldn't everything be shut down?"

"I'll give you a private tour. Afterwards I will take you to dinner, and then dancing if you like."

"Sounds like fun," Kara said, hoping to disguise her excitement.

"In fact," Omar said, "if you're tired of the rat race and would like a quiet night in, I can arrange for my chef to fix dinner at my residence, and we can take a tour of the consulate some other time."

Kara lifted her eyebrows and gave a wry smile. Omar blushed. "It's not what you think," he said haltingly.

"It's quite alright," Kara said, noticing Omar's embarrassment. "I rather like the idea of not having to compete with the motorized and pedestrian traffic indigenous to the city."

"Excellent. I'll have my chauffer pick you up about sevenish." Omar pulled two of his business cards from his breast pocket and handed them to Kara. "One is for you to keep. On the back of the other, write down your address and telephone number."

Turning one of the cards over, Kara said, "I'll give you my residence number and the number to my cell phone." After writing down the numbers, Kara returned the card to Omar. "I give my private numbers only to a precious few."

"I feel honored, my lady," Omar said as he kissed the card and placed it next to his heart.

"A bit dramatic, don't you think?" Kara teased.

"Can't you hear my heart throb?" Omar teased back. "Tonight is the first time I've sat next to a real live angel."

"I bet you say that to all of the women in your life."

Omar laughed nervously and said, "Only princesses."

"Are you referring to Princess Grace?"

"We never met. I'm talking about Princess Kara Isabella. The lady seated next to me."

"I didn't know you knew my last name."

"I make it a point to know all about whom I invite or intend to invite to dinner. I know you grew up in a castle, came from an influential family in Spain and are single."

"Speaking of marriage, how is it a perfect specimen of manhood like yourself has remained single for so long? Surely you have ten bodyguards on standby just to keep from being mauled?"

"Only ten?" Omar smiled, addressing the second question first.

"Okay, a dozen. You're avoiding the question aimed at your bachelorhood."

"Not really. Only once have I encountered a lady with whom I would be enamored enough to consider making the center of my life."

"And. . ."

"And I just met her tonight!" Omar said with a portentous look that melted any uncertainty Kara might have been harboring.

"Wow! You don't waste time do you?"

"Ah, I do not play cat-and-mouse. What's the advantage? Are you up to the challenge?" Omar asked.

"How can I not at least explore the possibility? But I have one request. Let's not move so fast. I need my space and time to absorb and evaluate what's happening. If you agree to let me have as much time as I need, I'm game."

"WONDERFUL! Absolutely wonderful. Take all the time you want. Ordinarily, I am not a patient man but in your case…." Omar said, raising his glass of wine and tilting it towards Kara. She responded by clinking her wine glass against his.

"Kara, Kara!" said Ambassador Madrid, trying to get her attention.

"Oh, Ambassador, I'm sorry. I was conversing with—"

"So I noticed. I was just telling Ambassdor Dupree about our import/export policy. Would you explain the details; I seem to be stuck trying to find the right words."

"Certainly," Kara responded nodding toward Ambassador Dupree. She turned and, having difficulty concentrating on the matter at hand, forced her attention to the French ambassador.

Omar smiled, thinking of how very clever he was to have ensnared Kara so easily into his web of deceit. What Kara did not know or even suspect was that Gabrielle was Omar's sister. Omar felt some discomfort at having deceived Kara, but his desire for revenge was more powerful than his conscience. He was, therefore, able to justify his motives. Under other circumstances, he could have been attracted to her, but he was not sure she hadn't played a role in Gabrielle's death, so he strung her along and didn't allow his heart to get in the way. He had to admit Kara fascinated him in other ways.

Saturday evening, Kara was ready when Omar's chauffer arrived on time. When she opened her door, the chauffer stood erect in a snappy navy-blue uniform, albeit without the tacky gold braid trim, his hat tucked under his arm. He introduced himself.

"Mademoiselle, I am Louis, Ambassador Omar Paulin's chauffer. If you need more time to prepare, I will wait in the limousine."

"Happy to meet you, Louis, I'm ready. Just a second while I grab my evening bag and I'll be right out."

"Thank you, Mademoiselle."

"Louis, unless you are required to be so formal, you may call me Kara."

"Thank you, Mademoiselle, but the ambassador prefers we use formal titles for his guests."

"Just between you and me, I think that's pretty stuffy."

"Whatever you say, Mademoiselle." Louis would die before he would dishonor his employer and friend, the ambassador, but he had to be polite, so he used one of his pat answers to acknowledge Kara's slam.

"We can go now, Louis," Kara responded. *I certainly hope the rest of the evening isn't going to be as tense and formal as my encounter with Louis.*

Omar's mansion was by far the most impressive structure among all of the ambassadors' residences in New York City. The home rose in the middle of seven expertly manicured acres with a wide paved driveway that led to a massive marble staircase leading to the entrance. An attractive olive-skinned woman opened the door as Kara approached. "Welcome to the Monacan residence." she said in perfect English and, sweeping her hand inward, gestured for Kara to enter. Kara stepped into the vast mansion, which was a balance of marble, stone and wood. The interior was meticulously detailed with marble floors polished to a mirror shine that reflected custom-crafted wooden doors and moldings. The two and a half story foyer was flanked by four marble columns and sparkled with stained glass windows set into the walls like gems. A massive Venetian crystal chandelier crowned the domed ceiling. The arc of the dome was adorned with delicate floral frescos.

As Kara moved further into the foyer, she was struck by the beauty of the appointments. A walnut octagonal table was positioned over an ebony medallion inlay in the marble floor of the sitting room. The table was adorned with a crystal vase of white lilies, simple but elegant. Kara's musings were interrupted as the servant closed the heavy oak door. "Ms. Isabella, may I take your wrap?"

"Thank you, but call me Kara. And what shall I call you?"

Kara still rankled at being called ma'am or Mademoiselle or Ms. Isabella. All of those titles made her feel older than her 26 years. She preferred her given name of Kara.

"My name is Frances, Mademoiselle."

"Frances? Is that a family name?"

"No, Mademoiselle. My parents were baptized Catholic by missionaries, and they wanted all nine of their children to be named after a saint, one the child could emulate."

"How quaint. You have eight siblings. . . ?"

Before Frances could answer, Omar strolled into the room, looking very handsome and casual in a white polo shirt, khaki Dockers and brown loafers.

"KARA! Come in, come in my dear."

Kara spun around and smiled warmly. "Omar, you have a lovely residence. I do not believe I've seen one as beautiful. It's even lovelier than the White House."

"You're too kind. Frances here is in charge of everything concerning the upkeep of the estate, and I compliment her on the fantastic job she is doing."

"Absolutely exquisite," Kara said. "Frances, you're a miracle. Let me know if and when you ever want a change of scenery, I'd love to have you on my payroll."

"Thank you, Mademoiselle," Frances said softly and exited the room.

Omar took Kara's arm and urging her forward, said, "Would you like to see the rest of the surroundings before we dine?"

"From the looks of it, that may take a while."

"Of course. Why don't we just relax and have a drink while Anthony finishes dinner."

"Let me guess. Anthony is Frances' brother."

"Why, yes. How did you know?"

"Frances told me she had eight siblings all named after saints so—"

"And here I thought you were psychic."

"Hardly, but wouldn't that be nice. Do all nine of the siblings work here at the residence?"

"No."

Kara stood waiting for further explanation, but it was not forthcoming. "I didn't mean to pry, I was only curious." She surprised herself at her interest in the family. It wasn't like her to be interested in anything that didn't directly relate to her. "I'm so sorry, please pardon me."

Omar took her arm and guided her into a large room adjacent to the foyer. The windows at the far end of the room presented a world-class view of gardens and a pond with a marble fountain. Omar continued, "I didn't realize you were so interested. To answer your question, I am only allotted five house servants and, of course, Louis. The other three house employees are, as you surmised, siblings of Frances and Anthony. They are Andrew, James and John. Andrew and James are gardeners and John helps Frances with the upkeep of the house. The other four siblings are still in Monaco, they work for the Church. They are indeed a special family, and I'm lucky to have them in my employ.

"The children were rescued by an international children's foundation in Nigeria when, unfortunately, their parents as well as the missionaries were slaughtered in a civil uprising. Miraculously enough the organization was able to keep the children together until they were eventually relocated. The children were not at the mission at the time of the massacre. They were in school so they escaped. But enough history. This is a special occasion and you, my dear, look absolutely ravishing."

Kara felt her face grow warm. *What is happening to me? I don't usually react like this. I'm always the one in control.* "Thank you, Omar. I believe you're making me blush."

"So I am and it looks lovely on you."

After they had dined on Anthony's famous roast lamb, Omar gave Kara a tour of the mansion. It was obvious no expense was spared decorating and furnishing the home. Omar designed the tour to conclude in the master suite on the third floor. Circumventing the bedroom, Omar escorted Kara through the sitting room. He took her hand and led her to the balcony, which overlooked the well-groomed garden at the rear of the estate. Fragrance from the flowers wafted up, a vague outline of the Statue of Liberty emerged through the mist in the distance, and the lights of the city were hypnotic. The evening was warm but not hot, and a cool breeze enveloped them as they stood looking at the panorama before them.

"It's breathtaking," Kara said in a soft voice. "I've never seen the city from this angle. Thank you for sharing this with me." She worried that Omar was moving much too fast and had plans of his own for the rest of the evening. "Dinner, the tour, and tour guide were exceptional. I have had a delightful evening." She glanced at her watch. "I really must go."

"Oh, so soon? There's so much more to see."

I just bet there is, Kara thought. "I have an early day tomorrow even though it is Sunday. I have several dossiers to read in preparation for Ambassador Madrid's Monday meetings. If I read them too far in advance, I tend to forget important points, so I've made it a habit of doing my homework the evening before the meetings."

"Very well, if you must, you must. I will call Louis and have him bring the limo around. I hope you will be kind enough to grace my humble abode with your presence again sometime soon."

"Humble abode indeed! And yes, I accept your invitation for a return visit. This has been a most enjoyable evening, and I look forward to our next," Kara said.

"Wonderful! I always live in fear that I will discourage visitors by saying the wrong thing at the wrong time. Although my language skills are strong, sometimes the inflection or double meaning of words can be misinterpreted."

"I know that scenario. But you haven't said or done anything wrong. You are a gracious gentleman, and I like being with you."

"You have made my day. On second thought, revise that to 'you have made my week.' Thank you for your kindness." At that moment, the limo drove up the circular driveway. "Oh, here comes Louis. Let me walk you down the stairs."

Louis stopped the limo and got out to open the door for Kara. Omar waived him off and opened the door himself. Holding her hand as she stooped to get into the vehicle, Omar pulled her into him and kissed her with a passion she had never experienced. When he stepped back from the embrace, she looked at him with wide, questioning eyes. *Maybe I was too anxious to leave,* she thought as she settled into the plush beige leather of the spacious back seat. She looked up at Omar and tried to read the expression in his eyes as Louis pulled slowly away.

🦢

Omar jammed his hands into his pants' pockets and watched the limo until it was out of sight, then he bounded back up the marble stairs and into the foyer. He smiled broadly. *Well, you international playboy you, I believe you've captured her.*

🦢

Kara hadn't given Mark a single thought all evening. With the city looming before her, she was jerked back into reality. Entering her apartment depressed her after being at the lush Monacan residence. *I lived a fairytale for a few hours. I could get used to that kind of life with that kind of man. No wonder Grace made the choice she did.* She suddenly became homesick for the luxurious life she had known in Spain. *Maybe I should forgive and forget.* But before she fell asleep, the vengeful side of her surfaced and she renewed her vow to exact revenge.

🦢

Mark had so much to cope with that he hadn't paid attention to the fact that he had not heard from Kara all weekend. He paced up and down in his apartment waiting for Simson to call. Every so often he would glance at his phone willing it to ring. He could stand the suspense no longer, so he called Simson.

Vern looked at the caller ID and opted not to answer. He wanted to give Cynthia as much of a head start as possible, but he feared if he didn't have an answer for Langford soon, the Senator would seek out someone else to do the investigation.

Vern knew Langford had access to the secret service as a United States Senator and being blackmailed made that service inevitable.

CHAPTER 12

THE BIGGER THEY ARE, THE HARDER THEY FALL

AS SOON AS CYNTHIA'S FEET hit the tarmac, she knew she had made the right decision. New Orleans felt warm and friendly; New Orleans felt like home. She had made a reservation at the *Inn on Bourbon* for the week. She wanted time to adjust and look for a job. She chose the *Inn* because it was located in the French Quarter, and there was a continuous barrage of parties up and down Bourbon Street. Cynthia welcomed the distraction. She stood on her second floor balcony and watched the revelers walk past, drinking, singing, laughing and loving. A couple of young rag-tag boys wearing tap shoes were performing under a streetlamp on the corner. They were actually quite good, and passersby dropped coins in a hat the boys had at their feet. A mime, his face painted white with heavy eye shadow and lips painted red, stood motionless in the middle of the block. Every so often, he would quickly change his stance but always outsmarted those trying to catch him moving. Cynthia loved being a part of the Big Easy. Although Mardi Gras was months away, she hoped she would be there for that celebration and prayed she would still be alive then.

Early Tuesday morning, Mark received a call from Vern informing him that he had nothing to report.

"What! You've got to be kidding. I thought you had the contacts and the savvy to produce results." Mark slumped in his chair, resting his forehead on his palm.

"It appears that the email was sent from one of those cafés that offer Internet service to their customers. Even if I could track down the source, it would be impossible to identify which patron sent the email. I'm waiving my expenses since I didn't produce any tangible lead, but I'm keeping the $15,000. I told you up front I couldn't guarantee results."

"That's robbery! How dare you. . ." Mark jumped up almost knocking his chair over.

Vern had hung up the phone.

Mark stammered and stuttered spewing saliva. Spent, he collapsed in his chair and rested his elbows on the desk, head in his hands. *What the hell, it was Kara's money but where do I go from here?"* He called Kara to give her the bad news.

"Hello," Kara chirped, thinking the call was from Omar.

"Kara, Simson struck out."

Kara flinched. Then masking her disappointment she said, "What? That surprises me."

"You recommended him. How is it you know such an unsavory individual?"

Kara didn't answer. She just sat there in disbelief.

"Kara? Kara? Are you there?"

"Yes." After a slight pause, she said, "You sound like you're at your wits end."

"I am. His cavalier attitude infuriated me, and when I tried to quiz him, he hung up on me. I don't know where to go from here?"

"Did he give any explanation?"

"No. When I became cross with him, he just hung up. After all, he's got his money. You really think he gives a damn about not having earned it?"

"Maybe it's just a personality conflict between the two of you. I'll call him and see if I can smooth this over."

"No! Forget it. I did nothing wrong and will not apologize to that raggedy-assed son-of-a-bitch! I don't want you interfering."

"Okay, okay. Have it your way. If you hear from the blackmailer again, what do you intend to do?"

"How should I know? I'm way over my head here."

"Why not enlist the Secret Service to look into it?"

"I really don't want to involve anyone else. I don't want this getting out."

"If you have nothing to hide, why would you care?"

"Kara, get real. It doesn't matter whether or not I have skeletons in my closet. Once my reputation is smeared, true or not, I'm toast. You know how John Q. responds to slander—they love to believe it, and there is nothing I could do to convince them otherwise."

"True, but don't throw in the towel just yet. Maybe the blackmailer got cold feet and decided to give it up. After all, it takes a lot of guts to blackmail a Senator and presidential candidate. Just exactly what did the blackmail note say?"

"It was a demand for money."

"Money in exchange for what?" Kara was beyond frustrated with Mark's evasiveness.

"I'm not really sure."

"You're not really sure! You're certainly going to great lengths to hush up something you're not really sure of. You can deal with this problem on your own. If you don't trust me enough to con-fide in me, I don't want to be involved. How do you expect me to analyze the situation if I don't know what the situation is? Good bye!" Kara then slammed the receiver down.

⟋⟍

Vern sat at his desk rolling a fresh cigar between his thumb and forefinger. He sipped a glass of bourbon. *If I'm correct, Kara will be calling as soon as she talks to Mark.* He barely had time to formulate the thought when the phone rang.

"Vern, you bastard, what the hell is going on?" Kara barked into the phone.

"And to whom am I speaking?" Vern said snidely, obviously enjoying Kara's agitation.

Kara didn't answer.

"Hello, mystery caller, are you there?" Vern asked in a grating voice.

"Cut the crap. I deserve an explanation. You're the one who claims to have all the answers."

"And, may I remind *you*, my services did not come with a guarantee. Bitch, you don't deserve anything."

"Okay, now that you have that out of the way, can we talk without insulting each other?" Kara said more calmly.

"Sure. What do you want to talk about, the weather?"

"Do you know who you're dealing with, Simson? Mark has a run at the White House. If he is elected. . .well, you fill in the blanks."

"*If* is the operative word here. What if the blackmailer has information that will destroy his chance of being elected along with his entire career? I don't know. I'm merely guessing. It takes guts to initiate something of this magnitude. Appears to me the blackmailer has the ammunition and is not afraid to start the war."

"You're the expert. What do you suggest Mark do at this point?"

"Oh, so now you want advice from the *bastard*?"

"Vern, just give it up. This is serious and, yes, I'm asking for advice."

"Okay, my advice is to wait and see what happens next. There isn't much Mark can do until he's contacted again. Remember, the first payment deadline has come and gone. When and if he gets contacted again, I'll take another look at it."

"Okay," Kara replied, relief in her voice. She didn't want Vern to desert them. Since Mark stubbornly refused to involve anyone else, Vern was all they had.

"Just relax and wait," Vern said. "Nothing can be done in the interim anyway, so there's no use getting gray hair over this."

"I guess not. I'll let you know if and when anything happens."

"Sounds good. Catch ya on the flip-flop. Bye now."

Kara began to wonder how high her blood pressure went each time she talked to Vern. He was the most infuriating man she had ever known.

With the election just months away, the Committee to Elect Langford was gearing up to do some serious campaigning. Their campaign slogan: *Langford – A Vote for a Better Tomorrow*, was emblazoned on billboards countrywide. Placards, business cards and letterheads also bore the slogan. With all the hype generated by his campaign, Mark pushed the blackmail threat to the back of his mind. After all, he thought, When I'm president, I can stifle my detractors. I will have the DOJ and the IRS in my pocket. Anyway, nothing may come of it. I may be worried for no reason. No guts, no glory. Mark spent many hours at his headquarters going over speeches and approving banners, posters, and various other documents. He would not allow detours to take him off course. His calendar was soon bulging with in-and-out-of-state appearances. A luxury bus was leased to provide transportation to locations both near and

far, and the hectic pace of campaigning encom-
passed his every waking moment. He had little
time for anything else.

Kara tracked Mark's progress through the
media and was pleased to learn that he was gaining on the incumbent. *The bigger they are, the
harder they fall. I want the privilege of bringing him
to his knees, and he won't have to look far to know
who wielded the sword.*

CHAPTER 13

The World, the Flesh and the Devil

KARA AND OMAR began seeing each other on a regular basis. Their interests dovetailed and they genuinely enjoyed each other's company. Unlike other wealthy men, Omar did not shower Kara with gifts. Kara didn't mind because she considered the time they spent together as a divine gift. They dined together almost every evening either at Omar's residence, or at UN functions they were required to attend.

One hot summer evening, Omar met Kara at the door of his residence. "I have a surprise for you," he said. He tucked her arm under his and escorted her to the limo waiting in the driveway.

"Wonderful! I love surprises!" Kara said as the two comforted themselves in the backseat of the limo.

Omar had arranged for Louis to drive them to the pier where *Raz 'Mataz*, Omar's personal yacht, was moored. Kara didn't know he had a yacht, much less one as large and luxurious as the one she now admired.

"Oh, my God. Is this yours?" she asked.

"One of my many toys. The water is my playground. Has been for as long as I can remember and continues to be. Hope you share the same passion."

"I spent many hours on a yawl as a teenager, and of course, my family's yacht, the *Mar Leon*. The *Leon* is moored at Costa del Sol east of Gibraltar, not too far from Madrid."

"Small world. On her maiden voyage, the *Raz* sailed from Costa del Sol up to Costa Brava. In fact, we spent several days in Barcelona sightseeing and enjoying the sunny beaches along the Mediterranean coast."

"Looks like we have similar tastes," Kara said as Omar helped her up the gang plank."

"I've arranged for Miguel, our captain, to take us for a cruise around New York Harbor, that is if you're up to it," Omar said, as the two boarded and were greeted by Miguel.

"I'm overwhelmed. I never expected such a fanfare. I should have brought a wrap. Once the sun sets, everything cools down especially once we're underway."

"Prepared for it." Omar pointed in the direction of the hall that led to the Admiral's Quarters. "Have a closet just for a special guest, should I be fortunate enough to have one, which contains everything that special someone would need."

Kara blushed. *This isn't his first rodeo,* she mused.

"Why are you looking at me like that?" Omar asked.

"Is my expression that transparent?"

"All I know is that you have that look on your face that my mother had when she didn't believe my excuses."

"Well?"

"My mother travels with me sometimes, and you're about her size."

"Nice save," Kara said teasingly.

"In case you're wondering," Omar said, "our chef is preparing a seafood delight to celebrate your first cruise aboard the *Raz 'Mataz.*"

It doesn't get any better than this, Kara thought as Omar gave her the royal tour, culminating in an inspection of the Admiral's Quarters.

Kara shivered in the misty breeze, so Omar removed his jacket and placed it around her shoulders. He gently turned her toward him and kissed her deeply on the lips. Before long, the two were lying on the king-sized bed, synchronizing their cadence with the sway of the yacht.

When Kara and Omar arrived in the dining room, Anthony was positioned behind the bar, fixing the ship's specialty.

"I will have the pina coladas ready in no time," Anthony said.

"Sorry about the delay," Omar said. "Something totally unexpected came up that required my immediate attention."

Kara felt embarrassed but not enough to blush or let loose of Omar's arm. Omar leaned down and whispered to Kara. "I do honor my priorities, you know."

"I could get used to that," Kara responded. "Is your dedication to detail and sense of duty a trait that defines you or is it contrived?"

"What you see is what you get. Come, our dinner awaits."

While they dined, Kara noticed that Omar was picking at his food and seemed preoccupied.

"Having second thoughts already?" Kara asked.

"Just embarking on a quiet trip," Omar replied. "Wondering if I'm infringing on someone else's territory."

Kara shook her head and squinted her eyes, "Do you think I'm a two-timer?"

"Not at all," Omar replied sheepishly. "The rumor mill has it that you and Mark Langford are an item. I just don't want to become a wedge between the two of you."

Kara was silent not knowing how to reply. She did have feelings for Mark, but the love she had for him had turned to hate and she now despised him.

"H-m-m-m, did I strike a nerve? Your silence is deafening. It's probably none of my business but. . ."

"No, no. That's all right. Just by stating that you didn't want to encroach on another's territory goes to your character. You are indeed a gentleman and I respect that, so I will answer your question. Mark and I dated for several months and eventually became engaged. We became intimate, but because of the STDs floating around out there, I insisted on being sexually exclusive. He agreed and often told me that we were monogamous. Then one day I found out he had another sexual partner, which was later confirmed. She may not have been the only one, but one was enough for me to end it. That's the long-and-short of it."

"I didn't mean to pry into your personal life, but thank you for sharing that with me," Omar whispered as he leaned across the dinner table and took both of Kara's hands in his. "Now I know the ground rules, and I will carefully guard my fidelity. I want you to believe that you can trust me. Langford must be a very foolish man to have let you slip through his fingers. This other woman he was seeing, what was she like? I can't imagine she, or anyone else, could even hold a candle to you."

Kara squeezed Omar's hands. "It doesn't matter anymore. Even though the other woman's out of the picture, I'm done with the likes of Mark Langford."

Seizing upon the opportunity, Omar said, "Oh, I see. What happened to the other woman?"

Kara just shrugged her shoulders not knowing how much she should share with Omar.

"Now I'm really confused," Omar pressed on.

Kara grew silent. She sensed she was getting the third degree and wasn't sure if Omar's intentions were focused on her availability. Omar appeared more interested in her competition then in her. Something didn't seem right. She was relieved when Omar changed the subject.

"Kara, I have to return to Monaco on business for a few days sometime this month. It's lovely there this time of year. Is there a chance you can take some time off and accompany me? I'll be gone only five days including the weekend."

"That sounds wonderful. I've never been to Monaco and I would love that, especially in the company of the ambassador himself. When do you plan on leaving?"

"I do not have set plans. What I have to do can be done any time within the month. I first wanted to invite you along and see if you could get away for a few days."

"Ambassador Madrid's calendar is open the last week of this month. I will ask him if I can take those days off. Does that work for you?"

"Absolutely. Let me know as soon as you can, so I can make arrangements."

Upon returning to work, Kara asked Ambassador Madrid about taking the last week of the month off as vacation. She told him she wanted to travel to Spain and see her family.

Ambassador Madrid smiled and peered at his calendar. "Of course. I have nothing during that week, and in fact, I will take advantage of the open time myself and take Alejandra on a small vacation. I've been wanting to visit Florida, and this sounds like the perfect opportunity. Those fancy hotels along the beaches have been haunting me ever since I arrived in the U.S."

Kara laughed. "H-m-m-m, I may change my mind and go with you and Alejandra."

"Of course, you're always welcome to join us, but I understand the need to see one's family."

As soon as Kara left the ambassador's office, she telephoned Omar on his private line.

"Omar, I've talked to Ambassador Madrid, and he has agreed to let me take the last week of the month off."

"Excellent! Since you have the whole week off, we can make it an excursion. As the Americans say, I shall get the ball rolling. I'll see you later at dinner? Anthony is preparing one of my favorite dishes, and I am anxious for you to try it. I'll have Louis pick you up at the usual time."

"I'll be ready. Until then."

Omar wasn't sure what Kara knew only that she knew more than what she was revealing. The trip to Monaco would be the stimulus that would engender trust and confidence and a willingness on Kara's part to confide in him. He was feeling somewhat guilty in masking his true intentions and, in effect, deceiving Kara. In his mind, his scheme was two-fold: to pry information out of Kara and at the same time experience sensual pleasure. The more time he spent with Kara, the more he was unsure as to which one had priority.

As the plane circled the airfield, the view of Monte Carlo was extraordinary, and Kara understood why Princess Grace was so taken with this country. The stucco residences crowned with red Spanish-tile roofs and generously landscaped were breathtaking. It appeared that everyone had a swimming pool. In the distance, Kara could see the French Riviera beckoning to them as they approached the landing strip. She gripped Omar's hand tightly and smiled at him then turned back to the window. The experience was surreal; like being on a movie set.

"Well, darling, what do you think so far?"

"I'm speechless. I'm eager to take in the sights including the French Riviera."

Omar raised his eyebrows. "I take it you're not at all inhibited about shedding your clothing."

"When I said take in the sights, I meant as a spectator not as a spectacle."

"Good choice," Omar said. "The hotels and casinos along the beach at the Riviera are enchanting. I will arrange for us to spend several days there just as you wish. By the way, if you want to test your luck, the gaming tables in the casinos are player friendly for the most part. Are you a gambler?"

"Not really, I wasn't old enough when we visited places where gambling was allowed, and besides my father taught me not to gamble unless the odds were in my favor. One of his mantras is, Don't risk a lot for a little."

Omar looked away for a moment, and his jaw clenched. "Well then, you will be my good luck charm while I take the risks."

"If you win, you'll have to split with me."

"And if I lose?"

"You're on your own."

Omar's residence was located on a hill overlooking Monte Carlo. A part-time staff consisting of a butler, maid and chef greeted Omar and his special guest upon their arrival.

"Welcome home, Ambassador," Xavier said. Omar shook hands with each of his staff members. Omar introduced Kara to his staff, and Kara spoke to them in perfect French.

Xavier assisted the limo driver in retrieving Omar and Kara's luggage. Standing in the foyer, Kara marveled at the grandeur of Omar's mansion. It was not quite as splendid as the Isabella estate in Spain but splendid nonetheless. There was a certain serenity about the setting—and Omar—that engulfed and enraptured Kara.

"Why don't we go in and have a look around," Omar said.

Omar showed Kara to a bedroom suite on the second floor that she would be using during their stay. The master bedroom was adjacent to her suite. Xavier deposited her suitcases in her suite. In French, he said, "Dinner is in one hour. That will give you time to settle in." Omar announced that he was going to freshen up and would stop by Kara's room and escort her to dinner. Once alone, Kara walked out onto the balcony and looked at the panoramic view. Monte Carlo was an exquisite city, sitting on craggy rocks rising from the Mediterranean Sea. No wonder it was host to royalty and some of the most dazzling entertainment figures in the world. Kara couldn't think of any place she would rather be.

She unpacked her clothes and selected black slacks, a cream-colored silk long-sleeved blouse and black ballerina slippers to wear to dinner. After showering and dressing, she carefully reapplied her makeup and put on a pair of gold

earrings along with her three signature pieces, a
gold peridot birthstone ring, a small gold cross,
and a gold watch. She examined herself in the
full-length mirror and was satisfied. One of her
mantras was, *Always look your best*. And so she
did—always.

During dinner, Omar regaled Kara with stories
of his life in Monte Carlo. However, he did not
include the part about the death of his parents and
having been raised by his maternal grandmother.
Nor did he mention his sister by name. If Kara
had asked, he would have told her. For now, he
would wait for the right opportunity to set the
bait and see if she bites.

"Let's take a walk," Omar suggested after dinner. "I want to show you around and show you off.
There is a little café not too far from here where
we can get a drink and mingle with the locals.
What's that saying, *Show, don't tell?* If I tell them
about you, they'll think I'm embellishing. If I
show them they'll be envious."

"That sounds like fun." Kara basked in the
unexpected compliment.

Omar held her hand as they strolled down the
hill and guided her into a small sidewalk café.

"Omar! You ole dog. Where you been?" the
waiter asked in broken English.

"Franco," Omar replied, giving the portly
good-natured man a hug and slap on the back.
"I've been in New York, you remember, the UN?"

"Ah, yes. I remember. We miss you here."

"And I miss all of you as well. There is no *Rouge* in New York or anything equal to it." He placed his hand on Kara's shoulder. "This is Kara Isabella who also works at the UN. She has graciously agreed to accompany me on this trip. It is her first visit to Monte Carlo."

"You speak French, mademoiselle?" Franco asked in French.

"Oui," she replied. "Pleased to make your acquaintance."

"And me, too, yours. Welcome to *Rouge*. Are all UN peoples pretty as you? If yes, I want go."

"You're too kind. Thank you for the compliment."

Picking up on the flirting, Omar jumped in and said, "No, you wanna-be-bandit. There are the usual assortment of dogs working at the UN. I just got lucky."

Omar winked at Kara and led her to an outside table. "Franco, we'll have my usual."

"Coming right there," Franco said, trying to sound American.

A slight breeze kept the evening cool. Kara sat at the outside table watching the passing crowd and mused, *I wonder how long this has been going on?*

"A penny. . ." Omar said.

"What?" Kara answered, snapping back into the present.

"A penny for your thoughts." Omar repeated.

"A penny? Haven't you heard of inflation? Thoughts now cost ten cents—each."

Laughing, Omar fished a dime out of his pants pocket and slapped it on the table. "There, now I want my money's worth."

Kara laughed and picked up the coin. Twirling it in her fingers, she answered, "I was just thinking of how very wonderful this place is and that I could stay here forever."

"Is that the truth or are you just saying that so I won't feel cheated it cost me an extra nine cents?" Omar tilted his head and fixed his gaze on Kara.

"With you here, I could stay forever," Kara said transfixed.

Omar reached across the table and caressed her hand. He was experiencing feelings for her that he wished he could suppress. They left the café and walked hand in hand back to Omar's residence where in the privacy of each other, they experienced the splendor of their first night in Monte Carlo.

The next morning Omar departed for Palais Princier de Monaco, but before he left, he ordered a limousine for Kara so she could take in the sights of Monte Carlo. When the limo arrived, Kara was ready and instructed the driver to show her the most captivating sites. They drove around for hours stopping here and there, so Kara could explore and mingle with the locals. The driver spoke French, English and some Spanish, so communicating was not a problem. He took Kara on a tour of Cannes, Antibes, Eze and Monaco proper. They also went to the Italian markets and ended up at some high-end boutiques where Kara shopped for clothing that would fit in with the local color, including the promised trip to the French Riviera. Kara reveled in mingling with the natives and chatting and laughing with the venders and street peddlers.

Kara did not see Omar again until dinner that evening, and when she did, she ran to him and leapt into his arms. She was wearing a cotton sundress with brightly colored flowers scattered about the aqua background, one she had purchased on her tour, a dress calculated to accentuate her attributes. She was bubbling over with excitement and couldn't wait to tell him about her day. She looked very Monacan. Omar took in a quick breath as he smiled approvingly.

"Hello, darling, I have had such a delightful day. I can't wait to tell you. . ."

"Well, just look at you. You've gone native and I am totally captivated. Come, let's have a drink before dinner, and you can tell me about your day."

Kara detailed the day's adventures. Omar laughed at some of her descriptions of the national treasures. He appeared moved by her little girl mannerisms, and his eyes conveyed an unmistakable meaning of reciprocated affection.

❧

Omar wasn't sure how long he could keep up the charade—not of his growing love for Kara which he'd finally acknowledged—but the real purpose of his having sought out Kara in the first place. He felt conflicted by the deceit, along with growing anxiety over his inability to solve the riddle of his sister's death.

After dinner the two again walked to town and ended up at *Rouge*. Franco opened the door for them with a smile and a warm greeting.

"Omar, my friend! Good to see you so soon again. How long you in Monaco?"

"We are going to the Riviera tomorrow for a couple of days and then back to New York. My UN term is up in two years, and then I plan to return home and, fair warning, you'll be seeing a lot of me. I miss Monaco and all my friends."

"I look forward to the day," Franco replied with sincerity in his voice. "And you, lovely lady, you coming back?"

Kara went wide-eyed. She didn't know how to answer that question. She looked at Omar for help. The moment was awkward so Franco finally said, "As visitor, I mean."

"Why, yes. I have fallen in love with Monaco, and I plan to return someday. I have one year remaining on my contract at the UN, and after that, I'm not sure where I'll be. A year is too far away to make plans."

When they returned to Omar's mansion after their evening enjoying the sights of Monte Carlo, Omar asked, "Do your future plans include marriage?"

"Not that I'm aware of unless you know something I don't," she answered.

"I do not have the proverbial crystal ball, but I sense there is someone special in your life."

"And who might that be?"

"I don't know, maybe Senator Langford?"

"I've already told you about him. Why do you keep bringing him up?"

"I guess I need reassurance that there's nothing there as you say. With the rumors floating around the UN, I must admit I'm skeptical. With his eyes on the White House and his being a United States Senator, I'm not much competition. You see, my fencing skills have deteriorated, and there is no way I could win a dual with him. . ."

"I thought duals went out with the dark ages. . ."

"I was just being sarcastic, my sweet. Of course, I would dual for your hand, any time anywhere. But first, you must convince me the prize would be completely mine. What happened between you and the Senator that caused you to make such a drastic decision?"

"What happened?" Kara overflowed with the hate for Mark that she had suppressed over the last several months. "The lying, cheating miserable bastard was two-timing me—or worse. I thought I told you that."

"Ah! You did allude to that. Do you know her?"

"She did my nails a few times. On one occasion, I overheard her talking to another technician about a Senator she was dating with details of their intimacy. She referred to him only as Mark, but the details sounded familiar so connecting the dots I put two-and-two together and, voilà, I came up with Senator Mark Langford. Unfortunately, she died a tragic death by falling from her fourth floor balcony."

"Do you think Mark was the cause of her death?"

"I don't know but I would rather doubt it. Mark is many things but a killer, I don't think so."

"If she was pressuring him, who knows?" Omar said. "He is a presidential candidate, and his reputation means a lot to him." Omar gave Kara a sidelong glance.

"Oh, come on, Omar. I can't see that. It just doesn't fit Mark. He's a philander and a coward. He wouldn't even confront the blackmailer. Can we drop the subject?"

"Of course. I was just curious, you know, like the cat. Did you say he was being blackmailed?"

Kara instantly fell silent. *My God, I don't believe I said that.* She faked a laugh. "Did I say that? My goodness, the tropical air must be affecting my brain. I have no idea where that came from."

Omar managed a smile and dropped the subject.

Sleep did not come easy for Omar. He had confirmed his suspicions about Mark and his romantic involvement with Gabrielle. However, unlike Kara, he was not convinced Mark was not the cause of Gabrielle's death. In fact, after his conversation with Kara, he was more convinced than ever that Mark was involved in Gabrielle's death. Originally, he thought it might have been an accident or, worse yet, that Mark had to silence

Gabrielle to avoid a scandal involving his sexual indiscretions. Now, Omar knew it was not an accident, and the real motive was, in all likelihood, Gabrielle's threat to expose Mark. Whatever the reason, Omar concluded Mark had to silence her once and for all. To make her death appear as an accident and divert attention away from him, Mark had pushed Gabrielle off the balcony.

The French Riviera surpassed even what Kara had expected, and her expectations were high. The Mediterranean was azure-blue, the sky was accented with fluffy marshmallow clouds, the weather was tropical, and the hotel was a palace unto itself. Kara stood on the balcony outside their hotel room, admiring the view from the tenth floor. She could see for miles an endless vista of beach, palm trees, ocean, and sky. It truly was a paradise. Omar joined her at the railing. Looking down, he remarked, "How terrifying to fall to one's death."

Stunned at the remark, Kara asked, "What brought that up?"

"I was thinking of the young lady that fell from the balcony, the one we talked about yesterday."

"Oh, Omar, can't we get past that awful situation. I don't want to be depressed, and I don't want you to be now that we're at the Riviera. I want us to be happy and have fun. Can we please?"

"Absolutely. I'm sorry I upset you. Let's change into our swimwear and stroll down the beach, catch some rays, and maybe take a dip."

Kara embraced Omar and ran back into the room. She snagged her bikini from a dresser drawer and headed for the bathroom. "Bet I beat you changing," she chided.

"No you don't, you little cheater. You got a head start but I'm a quick change artist and, look, I'm almost ready," Omar shouted struggling out of his trousers.

Kara wrapped a colorful beach towel around her waist as they exited their room and headed in the direction of the elevators. Omar wrapped his arm around Kara, and they rode down to the first floor. When the elevator doors opened, Omar took her hand and led her out onto a large patio facing the beach. There were multicolored umbrella tables scattered about and a Tiki bar off to one side. Omar pointed to a table, gesturing for her to sit while he went to the bar to get drinks. A pina colada always tasted better beachside. After enjoying the refreshing drink, they walked hand-in-hand along the sandy beach. They laughed and chatted as waves licked their feet. Kara tugged at Omar's hand, coaxing him into the surf, "Come on, you big baby. I won't let the sharks get you."

"They would more likely go for you, you look so delicious."

"Last one in becomes the minion of the other for a week," Kara teased.

"You're on," Omar said as he pushed Kara aside and caught the tide at its highest peak.

"You cheated," Kara said. The two clung to each other in the subsiding salty tide of the Mediterranean.

They dried off and strolled along the sandy beach, admiring the hotels along the ocean front. They were all extraordinary. After all, the businesses did cater to millionaires and billionaires. Omar had chosen the fabulous Le Meridien Beach Plaza for their stay on the Riviera. It was the choice of the rich and the famous, Omar had told Kara when they checked in.

Returning to their room, the couple showered and stretched out on the California king. Omar reached for Kara. "I'm not sure I like a bed this big," Omar said, "One could wear one's self out searching for his lover."

"Not to worry, darling. I'll find you," she answered in a sultry sexy voice and crawled into his embrace. The rest of the afternoon was spent loving and laughing.

Kara noticed as they dressed for dinner that the sun was setting. Sunset on the Riviera was quite a sight to behold. She quickly dressed and moved to the balcony, drinking in the panorama. Omar, looking very James Bond-ish in a black tuxedo, came up behind her. Kara had selected a peach chiffon dress with spaghetti straps. The skirt of the knee-length cocktail dress danced in the cool evening breeze. They stood drinking in the sunset, the sand, and the sea.

"Come, my lovely, I'm ravenous and our reservations are for seven thirty."

Kara had to be pried away from the view. As they entered the dining room, the couple commanded attention even in such a star-studded venue. Omar had reserved a table for two with an ocean view. Open sliding glass doors led to the outside patio, and a tropical breeze ruffled the tablecloth and embraced Kara's bare shoulders. The lights of the hotels along the beach twinkled in the water, and the ocean reflected rippling images of the towering structures as waves ebbed and flowed. Kara looked at Omar with different eyes. Whatever inhibitions or reservations she'd held were washed away by the waves of the Mediterranean. Was she falling in love?

Omar wasn't sure what he would do next as he was convinced Mark was involved in Gabrielle's death. He just knew it wasn't in his DNA to let such a deed go unpunished. For now, he would put everything on hold and sort it all out when he returned to the states. Until then, he would indulge in the delights of the world, the flesh, and the devil—and in the enjoyment of a beautiful woman, who could satisfy all three of those desires and more. Omar looked back at Kara with different eyes. He was falling hopelessly in love.

Kara peered longingly from the window of the plane as Monaco faded into the distance. She was torn between wanting to stay in paradise with this man forever and the urge to satisfy her lust for revenge. Omar took her hand in his and held it as the plane soared to 30,000 feet above the ocean on their return trip to New York.

"Did you enjoy your first visit to Monaco, dar-ling?" he asked, holding her left hand and toying with her birthstone ring.

Kara placed her right hand over his and answered, "It was everything I expected and more. There aren't words to describe how much I enjoyed a week in Monaco with. . ." Kara's voice broke and her vision blurred. Omar looked into her eyes. He slid his arm around her and pulled her close. She rested her head on his shoulder.

Louis was waiting when they arrived at Ken-nedy International.

"Ah, there you are and right on schedule. I have the limo parked just out front," Louis said as he and Omar shook hands.

"It's good to see you, Louis. How are things here?" Omar said as he handed Louis his duffle bag.

Taking the bag in one hand and one of Kara's carry-ons in the other, Louis responded, "Nothing exceptional happened in your absence. I assume you kept abreast of the news while in Monaco."

"Every morning. Is there anywhere on earth that does not carry CNN? News in the states seems to be news about everywhere else in the world. It follows me wherever I go. Can't hide from it. Ms. Isabella checked a *few* bags. It will take both of us to manage those."

Kara punched his arm and he groaned in mock anguish.

On the ride to her apartment, Omar sat with Kara in the backseat.

"I love you," Kara whispered to Omar.

"I love you, too," Omar whispered back.

When they arrived at Kara's apartment, Louis retrieved Kara's luggage from the trunk and carried it into the foyer of her apartment complex. He then returned to the limo while Omar walked Kara to the entrance of her building.

"Louis will see you to your suite. I will call you tomorrow." He kissed her and retreated to the limo.

Louis escorted Kara to her apartment, waited for her to unlock the door, and took the luggage inside. He didn't speak but did a quick walk through to ensure no one was lurking in the shadows. Being satisfied no one was there, he tipped his chauffer's cap and left, closing the door behind him. Kara heard him test the lock.

Once inside, she unpacked, placed the soiled clothes in a hamper, shed her travel clothing, and took a hot shower. Refreshed, she opened the shower door, toweled, wrapped a clean dry towel around her, and headed for her bedroom. On the way, she noticed the answering machine was blinking wildly. She could not even think of returning anyone's call that night so she ignored it, put on her pajamas, and crawled into bed. Pulling the sheet up to her neck, she thought once more of Omar and Monaco and fell into a deep satisfying sleep.

Monday dawned much too soon, and Kara groaned as she turned off the alarm. How she wished she could just snuggle down and go back to sleep, but instead, she staggered into the kitchen and looked into the refrigerator—pretty bare. She examined the pantry, looking for something quick and easy. There lurking before her eyes was a box of oats. Although not her favorite, Kara decided it was better than nothing. She was ravenous and prepared herself a bowl of cereal and took it with her to the bedroom. Holding the bowl in one hand and a spoon in the other, she sorted through her clothes. Nothing seemed right so she decided to wear the old standby, a black pants suit with a white blouse. One could never go wrong with black and white. She applied her makeup and left the building. Standing on the curb, she hailed a taxi. She couldn't even think of trying to navigate in traffic today.

The UN was swarming with visitors when she arrived. She breezed through security with the magic badge that allowed her access without scrutiny. She had forgotten this was United Nations Day, and visitors were crowding about the elevators. Kara stood patiently waiting for an elevator that wasn't packed to capacity. Finally, she was able to board and rode to the eleventh floor. As she got off, she breathed a sigh of relief. However, the situation at the Spanish Embassy was just as chaotic as it was in the lobby. *Thank God, it isn't like this all the time.*

"Kara, there you are," Ambassador Madrid said as he greeted her. "I thought you may have gotten caught up in the melee and carried away."

"Hello, sir. I was able to swim my way through and here I am. How was Florida?"

"Wonderful. We had a great time. How's your family?"

"Just fine. They send their regards," Kara responded. Then it was business as usual.

That afternoon Omar telephoned Kara. "Hello, beautiful! I miss you. How are you doing? Tired from the trip?"

"Hello right back at you handsome. Yes, I am weary but not necessarily from the trip. We have had a constant stream of visitors from the opening bell. Every so often when things quiet down for a minute I relive Monaco and feel exuberated. I had a wonderful time. Thank you so much for taking me."

"The pleasure was all mine. I know what you mean about the crowds. The Monacan suites have also been inundated. I, too, had a wonderful time and look forward to seeing you soon. But, may I suggest, after this day of horrors, we take tonight to recuperate and see each other tomorrow, same time, same place?"

"Sounds like a plan. I look forward to tomorrow." Kara hung up and smiled at the phone. *My love for Mark was nothing compared to my love for Omar. Spending my life with Mark would have been a huge mistake. Love is indeed better the second time around.*

CHAPTER 14

AN EYE FOR AN EYE

OMAR SPENT THE REST of the day sorting through what he knew and trying to discover what he didn't know.

"Louis, I briefed you last night on the ride home from Kara's. I feel we have enough to link Langford to Gabrielle's death. Let's take it apart piece by piece and see what we come up with."

"Yes, Sir. I, too, am very anxious to evaluate what we have." Omar knew what Louis would do if and when they determined Gabrielle was murdered. I certainly wouldn't want to be on the receiving end of Louis' wrath, he thought as he sat in silence, reflecting on the night so long ago when he and Louis had forced Antonio Sebastian's car over a cliff, the same cliff that claimed the lives of Omar's parents.

The two men hunkered down in Omar's office. "Since we are still assuming Gabrielle was pushed from the balcony, I want to proceed in that direction. If our investigation shows otherwise, we will then look at suicide or accident as the possible causes of Gabrielle's death. However, both of those scenarios seem highly unlikely to me. That just doesn't sound like Gabrielle. You knew she was acrophobic and wouldn't even venture to the railing, much less jump."

"I'm in total agreement." Muscular, tall, and imposing, Louis stood with one elbow resting on the mantel of the fireplace.

Omar looked up at his friend, "Here's what we know. Gabrielle was working at *BellaDonna* as a manicurist. She had numerous customers many of which were regulars. We were told by one of Gabrielle's co-workers that one of Gabrielle's customers was a United States Senator. Is that correct?"

Louis answered, "A co-worker by the name of Lacy Evans told me that Gabrielle manicured nails of a United States Senator she knew only as Mark. As a favor, she retrieved the appointment book for the month Gabrielle died and put a last name to the customer. It was Langford, Mark Langford. It also had his telephone number, which I checked. It was listed to him."

"Who determined that Kara Isabella was also a *BellaDonna* customer?"

"Actually," Louis replied, "while looking over Lacy's shoulder as she thumbed through the appointment book, I spotted Kara's name. At least for that month Gabrielle had done Kara's nails. Her first and last name and telephone number were listed."

"But Kara was actually Lacy's client and not Gabrielle's, correct?"

"When I spotted Kara's name, I asked Lacy if Kara was one of Gabrielle's customers, and she said no, that Gabrielle was just filling in while she was on vacation and that Kara was actually one of her regulars."

"I guess you already told me that. I was just trying to be precise. Now that I'm dating Kara, everything has taken on a whole new meaning."

"That's understandable," Louis replied. "Remember initially we thought it was only Langford who might have been involved in Gabrielle's death. When we discovered that he was dating both Gabrielle and Kara, we added Kara to the list."

Omar shook his head decisively. "I don't think Kara was involved. I'm not sure she even knew who the other woman was. Even if she did, I can't imagine she would eliminate the competition by such a heinous act."

"I'm curious about what transpired during your trip to Monaco. Before you left, you referred to it as a fishing expedition. Did you catch any fish?"

"Excellent question. The only thing of significance was that someone was blackmailing Langford, at least according to Kara. It appeared to me that she didn't realize the significance of that revelation. In fact, I don't think she meant to say it. She seemed flushed after she made the statement."

"Suppose Kara is blackmailing Langford?"

"No. It is more probable it was Gabrielle. After all, it was Gabrielle, not Kara, who was silenced."

"By the way, does Kara know that Gabrielle was your sister?"

"I never told her. I'm sure she doesn't even have a hint."

"What do you suppose her reaction will be when she finds out?"

"I don't even want to think about that."

Louis stared into space, wondering where it would all lead.

"Why so pensive?" Omar asked.

"Will you be offended if I become the devil's advocate?" Louis replied.

"You know I won't. You're just looking out for my best interests."

"I'm not ready to give up on the alternate suspect theory. Since jealously is a powerful motive, it is not farfetched to believe that when Kara found out about Gabrielle, she became enraged and took it upon herself to eliminate the competition."

"We were just down that road. If I hadn't just spent a week with Kara, I would harbor the same suspicion. I'm convinced Kara felt no animosity toward Gabrielle and realized Langford was the real culprit in the betrayal. Her ire was directed toward him, not my sister."

"It appears that is probably the case. Do you think Kara is part of the blackmail scheme?"

"To begin with, all we have is Kara's *faux pas*. We don't know for certain that Langford is being blackmailed. I doubt he would have confided in Kara, particularly since that would have generated still another witness who would need to be eliminated. If he was secretive about his affair with Gabrielle, don't you think he would be twice as secretive about his involvement in her death?"

"You're more than likely on target. I think both of us agree that if Langford is being blackmailed and, we identify the blackmailer, we have the means to determine once and for all whether Gabrielle fell to her death or was pushed."

"I will continue to probe Kara's blackmail reference. If she hadn't reacted the way she did to her Freudian slip, it wouldn't have piqued my interest. I doubt very seriously she is the blackmailer or even knows who the blackmailer is. However, I wouldn't put it past Langford to have disclosed the blackmail plot to Kara out of desperation or because he needed a cash cow to fund the hush money."

"Maybe it's just a matter of time before she confides in you and provides key pieces of the puzzle.

"I think she's on to me. She clammed up when I embarked on what no doubt appeared to her to be an interrogation. She'll probably tell me what she had to tell me in her own sweet time."

"I assume you want me and the boys to continue our investigation and do what we need to do to vindicate the death of Gabrielle?"

"Don't take any risks and remember, as far as everyone is concerned, I'm not in any way involved in your attempt to seek justice. In other words, everything you have done or are doing to unravel the mystery of Gabrielle's death, or will do, whether legal or illegal, is not and has not been orchestrated or sanctioned by me."

"You are well insulated. Nothing will point to you. I will continue to tell you only what you need to know, and the chickens, if they come home, will roost on my doorstep and not yours."

"Louis, you have and will continue to be a true friend of not only me but my family as well. I'm sure Gabrielle is up there looking down on us with loving approbation and appreciation."

"It's for her that we must pursue this to its logical conclusion," Louis said as he patted Omar on the shoulder.

"Time is not in our favor," Omar replied. "As they say, Justice delayed is justice denied."

Louis pressed his lips firmly and, with both eyebrows arched, said, "Langford can run, but he can't hide. His past will catch up to him sooner rather than later. Don't ask me how that will happen, just trust that it will."

Omar signified his approval by raising a clenched fist in the air followed by a thumbs up.

🦢

Louis had an edict—Spare no pain and take no prisoners.

When Omar told Louis of the blackmail Kara had let slip, Louis immediately began to formulate a plan. Louis knew from training and experience that blackmailers usually used the mail to contact their victims, so he decided to invade Langford's apartment while Langford was on the campaign trail and do a search. He wanted Herc, Mick, and Joseph to accompany him because of their varied skills. With these three men, Louis knew all the bases would be covered.

Louis was able to obtain Langford's itinerary online. Mark was campaigning in his home state of Indiana. He scheduled a three-city tour starting with South Bend in northern Indiana; Indianapolis, the capital of the state, located in central Indiana; and Evansville situated in the southern part of Indiana. This tour would take him three days, and that would give Louis' team enough time to breach Langford's apartment and conduct a very thorough search.

🦢

Mark was in his element. He loved campaigning: the attention, the excitement and the notoriety. The newspapers carried daily headline stories of his progress. The Hoosiers loved their Senator and came out in groves to spur him on. Mark was very handsome, and the women fawned all over him. The men also liked his style and pushed and shoved in order to shake his hand. It was obvious, at least to the residents of Indiana, that Mark would be the country's next President. The caravan moved across the state, and life on the campaign trail was so good that Mark gave very little thought to the blackmailer. He had the lock changed on his apartment door before he left DC, knowing Kara had a key. He also recognized that she was vindictive and would do everything she could to exact her perceived pound of flesh.

🦢

Carrying toolboxes and dressed in gray coveralls and baseball caps advertising Martin's Plumbing and Heating, Louis and his crew paused outside Langford's apartment. Surrounded by the other three, Joseph went down on one knee in front of the door. He quickly examined the lock, opened his toolbox and took a slim plastic pouch from within. Before anyone could bat an eye, the door swung open. The other three just stared as Joseph picked up his toolbox and entered the premises.

"Easy lock, hopefully the computer will be that simple," Joseph said to Mick.

"Nice digs," remarked Herc looking around.

"You and the ambassador been studying together?" Louis asked referring to Herc's use of American slang. Not comprehending, Herc just stared at him. The burglars had a master plan, and once inside, each man went about his assigned task. Mick, anxious to uncover a lead, went straight to the computer in the den and turned it on. Langford's screen saver blinked twice and then opened up to a seductive display of bikini-clad damsels playing volleyball on Malibu beach. "Hey, mates, lookie here," he beckoned. Thinking Mick had already found what they were looking for, the other burglars rushed to gather behind him. Herc whistled, Louis, breathing a sigh of frustration, bit back his disappointment, and Joseph just stared at the screen.

"Looks like our information about Langford being a playboy was correct. Wonder where one gets a screensaver of this caliber?" Joseph asked in a mix of jest and curiosity.

"Come on you heathens, although the view is delightful, we have a job to do. Get to it!" Louis ordered.

Joseph was assigned the living and bedrooms. He assaulted the rooms with a vengeance taking them apart piece-by-piece. Going through Mark's closet, Joseph stared at the array of suits that stood sentinel much like those on the racks in fine men's clothing stores. Some looked like they had never been worn. Joseph went through every pocket and squeezed all the linings making sure nothing remained hidden. All he found was chewing gum wrappers and lint. He emptied every drawer and examined every surface of every piece of furniture by turning dresser drawers upside down and searching in the vacant space occupied by the drawers. He combed the bed, linens and window coverings from top to bottom. He meticulously went through the living room, taking pillows up and running his hands along the fabric seams of each chair and sofa. He then turned the furniture over, carefully replacing them so that they appeared undisturbed. He looked under each ornament and leafed through all the books and magazines. The only thing he uncovered was dust.

Herc and Louis converged on the kitchen and bathrooms and took them apart, being careful not to damage any of the wood or fixtures. They mimicked Joseph's style of searching but, in the end, nothing of any significance was discovered.

Mick sat at the computer. He was in his element. Even with his excellent computer skills, it took him over an hour to figure out Langford's password, which turned out to be pretty simple. "*Abracadabra. Open Sesame* would have been my next guess," Mick mumbled. Once he had the password, he opened Langford's email and started through it.

After the rest of the team had finished their search, they put the apartment back as they had found it and joined Mick as he examined the emails on Langford's computer. Suddenly, he shouted, "By Jove, I believe we found something!" Once again, they grouped behind him and, looking over his shoulder, read the blackmail demand sent by Cynthia.

"Mick, run a copy. We'll take it back to the embassy and have the experts examine it to see what they can come up with," Louis said smiling.

"Right you are. Here we go," Mick replied as he set the printer into action.

Waiting for the printed copy, Louis asked, "Herc, is everything secure on this end?"

"All clear," Herc replied.

Louis took the copy Mick had just printed and put it in a manila envelope he had found in one of the desk drawers. He scanned the apartment, satisfied it was the way they found it. He then asked, "Mick, will Langford be able to detect you having hacked his computer?"

"Not unless he's looking for it. I don't believe the Senator has that kind of savvy."

They then exited as stealthily as they entered. They had found the golden egg.

Using his cell phone, Louis telephoned Omar. Although the hour was late, Omar asked him to bring the blackmailer's demand to his residence. When Louis arrived, he handed Omar the envelope, and they headed for the study. Omar took a seat in one of the chairs that flanked the fireplace and motioned for Louis to take the other. Louis stretched his legs and rested his head against the back of the chair content with the extraordinary find. It had been a long day but a productive day, and Louis savored every moment of the lull as he waited for Omar's reaction. Omar's jaw dropped as he read the note. His eyes lit up and he exclaimed, "This doesn't sound remotely like something Gabrielle would say. Her style of English is far different from the wording of this note. It's obvious she didn't write it. The question now is who did?"

"Sir, if I may, there are ways to find out who wrote it. The writer apparently knew about Langford and Gabrielle. That circle would be fairly limited. Also, there are ways to determine where the email originated."

"How long will it take to determine where and from whom the email originated?"

"Tomorrow I will take this to our computer lab at the embassy. They should be able to determine, at the very least, the location of the computer responsible for the transmission. That will be a starting place. We can then check Gabrielle's calendar and see if one of her clients resides at that location. Somehow we will be able to identify the originator of the email."

"Sounds like it's just a matter of putting two and two together," Omar said enthusiastically.

"Take heart," Louis said. "Just obtaining the demand note is one hell of a lead."

The next day Louis took the note to the computer lab at the Monacan embassy and instructed the head of the lab to determine the email's origin. At the end of the day, Louis was informed that they had a hit.

"Louis, we were able to isolate the origin of the note," Dr. Moulin said. "It was sent from one of the computers at New York University. Unfortunately, there are a number of computers available for use by students, faculty, and staff. Finding which one was used would not be as difficult as determining who used the computer and sent the email."

When Louis heard the note originated from NYU, he remembered Gabrielle's roommate, a girl he knew only by her first name, Cynthia, who was enrolled at the university.

"Dr. Moulin, you may very well have identified the originator of the email you just examined."

Dr. Moulin scratched his head. "I helped you find the needle in the haystack?"

"It appears that way. Thank you."

After leaving the lab, Louis headed straight to the Brookline Apartments, hoping that Cynthia had not moved away. When he buzzed the manager's apartment, Jim Wilson answered, "This is management. How can I help you?"

"Good afternoon. I'm trying to track down the former roommate of Gabrielle LaTana. Can you help me?"

"What's your connection?"

"I'm with the Monacan Embassy, and we are doing a follow up on Gabrielle's death. I represent the family. It does not appear the local authorities have made any progress."

"How right you are. That whole unfortunate incident has given this place a bad name. The owner would like to have it cleared. Come on in."

With that, Wilson hit the buzzer announcing that the door was unlocked. Wilson was standing in the doorway of the office when Louis stepped inside.

"It's nice to meet you, my name is Louis." Louis extended his hand.

"Likewise, you can call me Jim. Just what do you think about this whole affair? I have my own suspicions but that's all they are, suspicions."

"Would you like to share those suspicions with me? That may help us get to the bottom of this."

"Sure. Come in and make yourself at home. I was just going to open a beer. Are you a drinking man?"

"I'll join you," Louis replied. He didn't care for beer but quickly deduced drinking with Wilson would form a bond, and he wanted to squeeze every bit of information he could from the man.

Popping the cap and handing Louis the beer, Wilson gestured for him to sit in one of the chairs in front of his desk. Wilson sat in the other. After each of them had taken a sip of the brew, the manager commenced to tell Louis, "Well, it started about a year ago. This fellow, I later recognized him from his pictures in the newspaper as Mark Langford, the Democratic presidential candidate, started visiting Gabrielle on a regular basis. He would always come visiting when Gabrielle's roommate was at school. He—"

"Excuse me for interrupting, Louis said, "was the roommate's first name Cynthia?"

"Yes."

"What was her last name?"

"Sawyer."

"Any idea where she is now?" Louis asked, learning forward in his chair.

"Sorry, I thought you knew. Cynthia Sawyer was Gabrielle's roommate."

"Any idea where she is now?" Louis prodded, still leaning forward in his chair.

"Don't have the vaguest. After Gabrielle died, Cynthia disappeared. She didn't say a word to me, she just left. No forwarding address or anything. Just left. That struck me as being odd. But then I'm sure staying would have been hard on her, losing her roommate and all."

"How did the two get along?"

"They were as close as sisters. I could hear them laughing and carrying on in the pool, and I received some complaints from other tenants some evenings. Cynthia took Gabrielle's death pretty hard."

"Hum-m-m-m. Tell me more about Gabrielle's relationship with Mark Langford."

"Well, there's not much more to tell. I, of course, didn't know the nature of the relationship between the two, but I could guess. I saw him come and go for almost a year. What with her looks, you don't have to be a genius to connect the dots."

"Was he here the day she died?"

"Yes. I saw him come in. A few minutes later I heard them arguing on Gabrielle's balcony. You know the rest," Wilson said as he nervously twisted the beer bottle in his hand.

"Do you know whether Gabrielle fell or was pushed off the balcony?"

"I don't dare speculate."

"Is there anything else you want to add? This is all confidential, so you can speak your mind without worrying about how far it will go. You never know how important a scrap of information can be."

Wilson slowly shook his head. "I can't think of anything else right now."

"You have been very helpful, Jim. Here's my card. If you think of anything else, please give me a call. Gabrielle's family, as you can imagine, are beside themselves with grief and looking for closure. And of course that can only come when the issue is resolved as to whether Gabrielle fell, jumped, or was pushed to her death."

"I know she didn't jump," Wilson said.

Louis rubbed his chin. "Don't imagine you want to change your mind about not speculating?"

"All I can say is that she was too young to die."

The two men said their goodbyes, and Louis left the Brookline Apartments and went directly to the college. He located the Registrar's Office and went inside. A perky girl, probably a student in her early 20s, Louis surmised, raised her head from the book she was studying when he entered. She looked at him rather suspiciously and asked, "Is there something we can do for you?"

"I'm trying to locate a student. She was the roommate of my niece. My niece recently died, and I need some information I think her roommate may have. All I have is her name. Can you help me?"

"It's against the rules to give out personal information."

"Can you bend the rules a little?" Louis asked as he removed a hundred dollar bill from his billfold. He laid the bill on the counter that separated him and the receptionist. She looked longingly at the bill and finally said, "What's her name?"

"Cynthia Sawyer."

"Cynthia? Oh, I knew her. We were in computer classes together. I also knew your niece. The three of us would see each other at *Cal-Mars* on Friday nights on occasion. Cynthia didn't drop any classes or even say goodbye—she just left."

"You don't think Cynthia had anything to do with Gabrielle's death, do you?"

"Heavens, no! The two were very close and socialized together even though Gabrielle was not a student. Gabrielle seemed very involved in Cynthia's life and vice-versa."

"Why do you think Cynthia dropped from the face of the earth?"

"Shortly after Gabrielle's death, I spoke with Cynthia after one of our classes together. She seemed nervous and was fearful that what happened to Gabrielle would happen to her."

"Did she tell you what she thought happened to Gabrielle?"

"She just said she knew it wasn't an accident."

"Did Cynthia have friends here at school?"

"She didn't seem to socialize much. She had a job as well as attending school so that left little time to fraternize. I'm sorry, I'm not much help."

"You've been a lot of help," Louis said as he handed her the hundred-dollar bill. "Thanks again."

"Oh, no, thank you." She folded the bill and stuck it in her pocket.

On the way home, Louis began putting pieces of the puzzle together using tidbits he had gathered. He knew that Cynthia was Gabrielle's roommate. Being a computer student, she had the means and opportunity to send a blackmail note to Langford. Her motive was obvious, to extort money from the rich Senator. She obviously knew of the intimate relationship between Gabrielle and the Senator. It was highly unlikely that the good Senator would continue his liaison with Gabrielle once he was nominated, so he decided to break it off with her. Louis, knowing Gabrielle, correctly surmised she wouldn't take the news lightly and probably had an argument with her lover, culminating in her either falling or being pushed off the balcony. The question boiled down to whether Gabrielle's death was an accident or something more sinister. For the latter, a heavy penalty would need to be exacted. Just what that penalty would be, Louis was not quite sure.

꧁

When Rosa announced Louis, Omar told her to hold his calls and to send Louis in immediately. Since such visits were rare, Omar knew what Louis had to report was of some urgency.

Louis positioned himself at the corner of Omar's desk and disclosed to him what he had learned. Omar listened intently, and after pausing to absorb all that Louis had revealed, he finally spoke. "I cannot impose sentence on someone who may very well be innocent. I need proof that Senator Langford deliberately pushed her. Otherwise, I could not live with my conscience." *I'm still trying to get past what we did to Sebastian.* "So, here we are at an impasse. I suggest we sit tight. When the Senator returns from his campaigning, perhaps you and Herc could pay him a visit."

"Indeed, sir, that would be our pleasure."

꧁

Omar called Kara. He was convinced Kara had nothing to do with his sister's death. His intentions became more honorable. He wanted to seriously pursue Kara. He actually wanted to marry her.

"Hello, beautiful," he opened.

"Hey, handsome. I was hoping you would call."

"You were? Why is that?"

"Since your memory is so short, I guess I'll just have to show you—again."

"Oh! When can we begin?"

"You're the one who called me, so that's up to you."

"The sooner the better. I'll have Louis pick you up promptly at seven. That should give you time to get home and change into something more comfortable—and easy to remove."

"Why don't I just come naked?"

"Would you?"

"You're incorrigible. I'll see you this evening," Kara said feigning disgust.

Despite the disappointing events of the day concerning Gabrielle, Omar was in high spirits. He was falling in love and he loved it. Kara was the epitome of everything he ever wanted and more. He looked at the clock, four more hours. It seemed like an eternity.

Omar had an errand to run before dinner, so he left the office early. However, he arranged to be home when Kara arrived. He opened the door before she had time to ring the bell and said, "It was almost worth the wait."

"Why 'almost'?" Kara queried.

"Every minute without you is pure torture."

Kara looked innocently behind her. "Are you addressing me?"

"Get in here you little vixen. Of course, I'm addressing you."

Kara didn't know or understand the cause of the transition, but she liked it. Omar embraced her and kissed her lightly on the neck. She responded by kissing him full on the mouth. He pushed her back and looked into her eyes; he saw something he hoped he would see, unremitting love. That afternoon when he decided to propose to Kara, he hoped Kara would be as excited about the ten-carat diamond as he was when he purchased it.

"Come in, Anthony has prepared a special dinner in your honor."

"Really, why in my honor?"

"From now on everything we do will be in your honor."

"Omar, I'm flattered but I don't understand."

"Oh, it's just my romantic nature. I have something for you, but you will have to wait until after dinner," he taunted.

"In that case let's get to it. I'm ravenous."

Omar had made a visit to a candy store/factory, *Sweet Surprise,* after purchasing the diamond ring. He picked up a five-pound box of chocolates and approached the clerk.

"Pardon me. I would like to ask a favor. I'm going to propose marriage to someone very special and want the occasion to be memorable. I would like to place this diamond ring in the center of the box so that when the lady opens the candy, walla! In order to do so, I would have to have the box rewrapped so she doesn't suspect anything. Would you rewrap it for me?"

"That's against company policy," the disinterested gum-chewing clerk said. "I could get fired for doing that."

Omar anticipated as much so he opened his wallet and extracted $20. "How about now?"

"You got yourself a deal." The clerk looked around to see if anyone was watching. Omar watched through the window separating the factory from the shop. The clerk pulled out a chocolate cream from the center of the box and, after removing her chewing gum, popped it into her mouth. She then took the tiny sponge pillow from the ring box, inserted it in the vacated spot, and pushed the ring into the slot in the pillow, displaying the diamond in its entire splendor. She held the open box up for Omar's approval. Under the bright lights in the factory, the diamond sparkled like the North Star on a clear night. Omar smiled, nodded his head, and gave the clerk a thumbs up. He was pleased.

The clerk rewrapped the chocolates in the shrink wrap and gave the box back to Omar. No one would suspect the box had been opened, Omar surmised. Omar paid for the chocolates and then gave the clerk an extra twenty. The clerk was all smiles as Omar left the shop and yelled after him, "Hope the ruse works!" Omar hoped so, too. He had not felt this way since he pinned his college sweetheart. Wonder what happened to my Sigma Chi pin, he thought as he headed for the parking garage.

After dinner, Omar pretended he had forgotten the surprise. Kara decided she could play along, at least for a little while to see where all this was going. She loved surprises and didn't want to spoil whatever he had planned. When he saw she remained patient, he finally said, "So, aren't you a little curious about your surprise?"

"More than a little but you're driving this bus so I'm trying to be polite. Are you going to tell me or do I have to break every bone in your body. . . ?"

He took her hand and led her to where Frances had placed a tray of wine and a crystal platter of beautifully decorated petit fours on the coffee table in front of the fireplace.

"Sit here by the fire, my love."

Kara dutifully positioned herself on the over-sized sofa. Omar sat next to her and produced the box of candy.

"This is for you. I know how you love chocolate."

"This is the surprise you've been taunting me with all evening?" Kara was more than a little disappointed.

"These are very special chocolates. You must open them, so we can try one. I was told these are to die for. . ."

Kara looked at the box. It was from a local candy factory so how special could they be? *Okay, I'll play his little game,* she thought as she tore the wrapper from the box.

"There, now are you happy?"

"But we must try one."

"Dinner was so wonderful, I don't know if I have room for even one chocolate. Besides, Frances has prepared those lovely petit fours, and I would not want to hurt her feelings by refusing to partake of them." It was her turn to torment him.

"Okay, we can have them later. May I pour you a glass of wine?" Omar said somewhat annoyed.

Kara picked up on his irritation and decided to relent. "Well, they smell awfully good, maybe just one. . ." she said, opening the lid. She saw the diamond twinkling in the light of the fireplace and squealed. She looked into his eyes, "Omar, I don't know what to say."

"Why don't you try yes?" he suggested, taking the ring out of the sponge and placing it on her finger.

"I'm not sure. After what happened with Mark. . .I thought I was in love with him. At the time Mark proposed, I thought he loved me, too. He bought me an extravagant ring, but I wasn't allowed to wear it or even tell anyone of our engagement. I. . .I. . .I now feel like Mark just used me. He knew Daddy was wealthy and had worldwide connections and could help him become elected by pulling strings and calling in favors. I. . .I don't want to be hurt like that ever again, I'm just not sure. . ."

"Kara, I'm not with you because of what you can do *for* me. I'm with you because of what you do *to* me. You're the rainbow after the rain, the calm after the storm, the light at the end of darkness—you're my everything."

Tears filled Kara's eyes and, looking into Omar's loving eyes, she whispered, "Yes. . . yes, yes."

Exhausted but exhilarated, Mark opened the door to his apartment. He felt the campaign was going well, and after his three-day tour of Indiana, he was fairly certain he would be nominated by his party. He was also gaining in the polls. He had been gone ten days, and was eager to return to his home where he could rest and be brought up to speed on what he had missed. He went immediately to his computer to see if he had a follow up email from the blackmailer. Much to his delight, he didn't. *Maybe, just maybe, this nightmare has ended.* He didn't take time to look at the rest of the emails. That could wait. All he wanted was a hot shower and a good night's sleep in his own bed.

Before taking a shower, he went to the refrigerator to find something for a quick snack. He had dinner on the plane but that was hours ago. A wedge of cheese caught his eye so he decided to have some cheese and crackers. He reached for a knife to slice the cheese, and he noticed the knife he selected was placed backwards in the block. He always placed knives with the handgrip indentions facing outwards. That way they were easy to grab. He surmised he probably did it when he was getting ready to leave for the campaign tour. He was excited so it wouldn't surprise him if he had. He took his snack and a cold beer into his bedroom and began to undress. The bed was perfectly made; this was not his doing. He never made a bed perfectly. The hair began to rise on his neck as he realized someone had been in his apartment in his absence. *I changed the lock on my door, so I know it couldn't have been Kara. Does the blackmailer have access to my home?* All of a sudden, his euphoria changed to anxiety. *How much of this can I take?*

Then he noticed movement in the dark corner of his bedroom, "Welcome back, Langford," a voice foreign to him said.

"Wh…wh…who are you and how did you get in here," Mark stuttered.

"Hold on there. I'm asking the questions."

Just then another figure appeared from the shadows and approached Mark. He was wearing a ski mask, and Mark realized immediately he was in big trouble. He dropped his beer and the plate of cheese and crackers onto the carpet and felt the cold of the beer spill.

"What do you want?" he asked, his voice trembling.

"We'll not hurt you if you answer a couple of questions truthfully. However, I must caution you; we know some of the answers, so if your answers don't jive, we have ways of extracting the truth."

"Who sent you? Was it Ballard?"

"Who's Ballard?" the first man asked. "Oh, yeah, he's the guy running against you. No, definitely not Ballard."

Mark stayed quiet. He didn't know what to expect, but he was terrified.

"We'll get right to it. What was your connection with Gabrielle LaTana?"

"Gabrielle? Is that what this is all about?"

"I'm asking the questions. Answer!"

"I knew her from the salon, *BellaDonna*. She manicured my nails occasionally."

"Wrong answer," came the reply, followed by a painful blow leveled by the second intruder to Mark's ribs. Mark howled in anguish.

"You want to try again?" the questioner asked.

Tears filled Mark's eyes from both pain and fear, "I was seeing her. We dated for a few months, that's all."

"Were you involved in an intimate relationship?"

Mark cringed. *How should I answer that?* Suddenly the pain in his ribs reminded him that he had better tell the truth.

"Yes."

"And. . .?"

"I don't understand."

"And what else?"

"Nothing else. I was never serious about her. I think she misinterpreted our relationship and had unrealistic expectations."

"What a convenient choice of words. Were you there when she fell to her death?"

"Yes." Mark groaned. "I went to see her to break it off. She became angry and ran out the sliding glass doors, stumbling over a wrought iron table and fell over the balcony railing. It was an accident. There wasn't anything I could do to prevent it, it happened so suddenly. I've been haunted by the sight and sound of her plunging to her death ever since."

After a brief pause, the questioner replied, "I'm inclined to take you at your word on that, but if I find out you lied, we'll be back."

"I'm not lying, I swear."

"You're a politician, so swearing doesn't mean a damn thing in your line of work."

The two men left the apartment slamming the door behind them. Mark went to his knees and wept. *Would there ever be an end to this nightmare?*

The next day proved to be just as confusing. Mark hadn't slept. He called Kara as soon as he was sure she would be up. He didn't have anyone else to turn to.

Kara answered the phone thinking it was Omar. "Good morning, darling. How did you sleep?"

"Not worth a damn," Mark replied.

Kara flinched when she heard Mark's voice. She wasn't expecting him to call for several days. "Mark, when did you get back?"

"Last night. It sounded like you were expecting my call."

"Oh, that. When I saw your number on the caller ID, I knew it was you," Kara lied. *Good grief, now what do I do? How am I going to tell him I'm engaged to another? I'll just let him think things are status quo until I'm better prepared.*

"Kara, two thugs attacked me last night in my apartment. They were there waiting for me when I got home. Do you think Simson had something to do with it?"

"Were you hurt?"

"Not really, but I was threatened."

"Why on earth would you even consider Simson? What reason would he have? Really, Mark. You're losing it!" *It appears as though I've dodged a bullet and just in time. Someone is really out for him.*

Mark replied, "I know, I know. I just don't have anywhere else to turn. Can I see you tonight?"

"Ahhh, I have plans so tonight is not good. Maybe later on in the week. I'll call you."

"But I need you now! Don't you understand my life is in shambles?"

"Looks to me like you are doing pretty well campaigning. Your numbers are up. How does that equate to your life being in shambles? Just forget the attack; it was probably hoods looking for drugs."

"Actually it wasn't hoods looking for drugs. It was hoods looking for some answers to Gabrielle's death. They alluded to the fact that I may have had something to do with it."

"Really! Why would they track you down of all people?"

"Because she manicured my nails once or twice? I don't know."

"Sounds to me like there was more to it than doing your nails once or twice. In fact, I'm inclined to believe that all of those 'Oh, by the way, honey, I have a dinner meeting with my committee tomorrow night. . .blah, blah, blah' you so innocently sprung on me so many times were actually rendezvous with Gabrielle. It occurs to me you always waited until the last minute to tell me in order to minimize the *pissed off time*. And you want me to protect and comfort you, now that you're the needy one. I don't think so, Mark. You broke my heart over and over again. You managed to kill all the good feelings I had for you. You know, you can't make someone fall in love with you, but you sure can make someone fall out of love with you. As far as I'm concerned, you're on your own. Don't bother calling me again. We're through." Kara hung up the phone without waiting for his response. *Well, that worked out pretty well. At least now he knows I'm no longer available. What he doesn't know yet is his political career is over. Wonder who the thugs were that attacked him. Interesting. . . I hope he experiences some of the hurt and misery he caused me over the course of our relationship with his lies and infidelity. He deserves that and more . . . much, much more.*

CHAPTER 15

WHAT GOES AROUND

KARA DUMPING HIM was almost more than Mark could handle in his current state of mind. He didn't even want to think of what *Daddy* would do when he found out. *Hell with both of 'em. I've spent most of Daddy's money, so what'd I need him for? When I win, she'll come running back. I'm sure of that. I gotta concentrate on the campaign and can't waste time trying to soothe her over—again.* Mark put the events of the morning aside and began working on his acceptance speech. After all, he had won his party's nomination to run for President. Everything else paled in comparison.

Kara and Omar were almost inseparable. They spent all of their spare time together. The evening after her conversation with Mark, Kara went to Omar's for dinner. Because of their open and honest relationship, Kara was compelled to tell Omar more about her relationship with Mark.

She had already told him about their intimacy, how he lied, deceived her, and betrayed her trust. There was more Kara wanted to divulge. "There's something I must tell you."

Omar stiffened. He was afraid that what was coming would destroy their relationship.

"You can tell me anything, my love. What's bothering you?"

Kara told Omar about the time she overheard Gabrielle talking to Cynthia at the spa during her manicure appointment. She also told Omar about having Mark followed to be certain her suspicions were correct.

"I thought I was in love with Mark. I didn't want to spoil our chance for happiness by jumping to conclusions. Now that I know what real love feels like," she said, squeezing his hand, "what I felt for Mark was probably infatuation." She concluded by telling Omar about the pictures she bought from Vern with a price tag of twenty-five thousand dollars and of her intentions to use them to destroy Mark's chances of being elected President.

Omar listened without interrupting. He wasn't surprised to hear all of this as he had surmised most of it. Kara having pictures, however, piqued his interest,

"You said you have pictures. I'd like to see them," his voice cracked when he thought of Gabrielle lying dead on the pavement.

Kara picked up on the emotion in Omar's voice. "Of course. I'll bring them tomorrow night." She saw the sorrow on his face. *What's going on?*

"Yes! Please do, I want to see them. Kara, you've been honest with me even though I sense it must have been difficult for you to tell me all of that. I love you even more, if that's possible, for doing so. Now I have something to tell you, and I hope you understand me as I have understood you."

"Omar, what is it?" Kara was fearful this was all going to end badly for her.

"Please be quiet and listen. First, I must tell you Gabrielle was my sister."

Kara gasped and jerked around to look him full in the face. "Your Sister? But how. . ." Tears streamed down her cheeks.

"Quiet my love; it's my turn to be Shahrazad. Knowing that Gabrielle was my sister, you will be more open to what I'm going to tell you."

Kara felt more for Omar than herself. She listened intently.

"When we learned of Gabrielle's death, we, that is Louis and I, knew we had to find out what happened. Gabrielle was like a sister to him as well.

"I was never satisfied with how the NYPD was handling the investigation, so I assigned my people to investigate Gabrielle's death. From her letters to our grandmother, a scant few I might add, I surmised she was dating a Senator. Louis and I naturally assumed he might have had something to do with her death. We also learned she had a roommate that went to NYU. Those were the only two leads we had plus her salon appointment book.

"Long story short, Louis broke into Langford's apartment and found the blackmail demand on his computer. We had our lab examine it, and they determined it came from the computer lab at NYU. So, two and two make four. It was then obvious to us that Gabrielle's roommate was the author of the extortion demand. We tried to find Cynthia, that's her name, Cynthia Sawyer. She just disappeared. That looked suspicious so Louis poked around at the university and discovered Cynthia was working at the time of Gabrielle's death, which cleared her of any involvement. Having also eliminated you, that left only one suspect that could have a motive to want Gabrielle out of the way. We now pretty much know how everything happened. The unanswered question is 'Did Langford push her or was it an accident as he claimed?' I've witnessed how emotional and unreasonable Gabrielle can be, so an accident is not impossible. She could easily have fallen in a fit of rage. Now you know why I must see the pictures."

Kara stared at Omar in sadness and disbelief.

"Forgive me, darling, but I used you to get information regarding Langford. That is, at first. I didn't intend to fall in love with you, but it happened. I'm thankful you came into my life. You're the best thing that ever happened to me. Believe me, Kara, everything I've said during and since our trip to Monaco has been from the heart. I love you more than life."

When Omar finished they both sat drenched in tears. Omar was determined to let Kara make the first move. If she wanted to end their relationship, then he would have to accept that. Finally, Kara took Omar's hand.

"Omar, we cannot let this come between us," she said. "If anything, it should make our love for one another stronger. Now everything makes perfect sense."

Omar sobbed uncontrollably. He was relieved
that everything was out in the open. Kara slid off
the sofa and knelt before him, encircling his waist
with her arms. Omar impulsively picked Kara up
and held her in such a tight embrace she could
scarcely breathe. Kissing each other on the face,
neck, and lips, they tasted the salty tears that neither could control.

Kara Isabella's lust for retaliation was still alive
and well, albeit not to the degree it had been
before falling in love with Omar. He meant more
to her than anything, and she was willing to sac-
rifice whatever it took to be with him. Regaining her composure somewhat, she said, "Omar,
I'm still not satisfied. I want Mark to pay for his
treachery. Am I wrong? Tell me darling what do
you want me to do, and I'll obey. I don't want to
destroy us over this. And are you certain you want
to see the pictures? They're pretty graphic."

With Kara sitting on his lap, Omar gently
stroked her back. After a few thoughtful seconds,
he finally spoke. "Yes, I must see them now that I
know they exist. I, too, want to destroy him. Even
if Mark didn't actually push my sister, he was at
the very least indirectly responsible for her death."

"Since we have the pictures, we can wait until
he gets the nomination and then release the pictures to the press. There are no guarantees that a
newspaper would print them nor is there a guarantee that they would deter the public from voting
for him, but it's all we have. What do you think?"

"I think the twenty-five thousand you spent on the pictures was a wise investment. I also think Americans are fickle enough to condemn him for his philandering and not vote for him. As you say, it's all we have so let's use it. What have we to lose?"

The convention center took on a life of its own. Red, white and blue bunting hung from the ceiling and garlands of red, white, and blue were tastefully strung throughout the hall. The stage was carpeted in blue with red and white accents. The arena was packed with revelers shouting and cheering. The delegates were hyped and waved *Langford—A Vote for a Better Tomorrow* placards. It was so noisy that it was difficult to hear the person next to you. President Winston F. Warrington was term limited, and Vice President Bartholomew Morrison had opted not to run. They both, however, enthusiastically supported Mark. VP Morris would make the nomination.

Morris strolled out onto the stage, and the crowd went wild. It took several long minutes to quiet the delegates down long enough for him to make his nomination speech. When he finally had their attention, he spent almost ten minutes detailing Marks accomplishments and qualifications. In conclusion, he said, "It is now my distinct honor to place in nomination the name of Mark Langford as the man best able to serve our great nation."

Mark's fellow senator, Pierce Fenning, received a raucous applause when he stepped forward. He also extolled Mark's virtues and concluded by saying, "I enthusiastically second the nomination of Mark Langford as the next president of the United States."

When the chairman asked if there were any other nominations, the delegate from Rhode Island arose and shouted, "I move that nominations cease and that Mark Langford be designated by acclamation as our party's nominee for president of the United States."

When the chairman banged his gavel and announced "Motion carried. Mark Langford will be our party's nominee for president of the United States," the crowd erupted. No amount of coaxing by the chairman calmed the assembly. Order was restored only after the delegates had their fill of celebration.

In the midst of the fanfare, Mark had walked onto the stage, poised to make his acceptance speech. When the chairman turned the podium over to him, the crowd again erupted with thunderous approbation. Through great effort, Mark was able to quiet down the crowd with animated hand gestures.

"My fellow delegates," Mark began, "I am humbled by your show of support and pledge to prove you correct in selecting me to be the candidate to lead our party to victory in November. We are the party of the people, and our party is all about parity and giving everyone an equal opportunity to succeed. We are not, as some suggest, a party asking for handouts and taking our fair share without giving our fair share in return. Nothing is free, especially freedom.

"We have learned from the mistakes of previous administrations and know that if government takes away incentive, it takes away initiative. If it takes away initiative, it takes away ambition and pride. And when government takes away ambition and pride, it takes away will and ultimately freedom. I promise that *none* of that will happen under my watch."

Mark went on to outline his plan to ensure a better quality of life for everyone "now and for generations to come."

Then he concluded by saying, "It has been said that Nero fiddled while Rome burned. Never will it be said that America decayed while I played. In fact, after I have served two terms, like the mythological Phoenix, America will rise from its ashes and be that shining nation, a beacon for the world to seek and emulate once again. This is not just a promise, but a guarantee."

Bedlam reigned in the convention center, registering 8.9 on the Richter scale as the traditional red, white, and blue balloons floated down from the rafters and filled the air with a symbol of hope and excited expectation.

Kara and Omar were transfixed as they watched the TV screen, wondering how it was that Mark could fool all the people all of the time.

"He's a fraud," Omar said as he shook his head. "Yet he has everyone eating out of his hand. What's his secret?"

"Ask Ted Bundy," Kara replied, pleased with the analogy.

"At least Bundy paid for his sins with his life," Omar said.

"Might happen to you-know-who."

"Don't even tease about it."

"You never know when your time is up."

"The clock is ticking."

As she promised, Kara showed Omar the photographs taken at the time of Gabrielle's death the following evening after her confession of having the pictures. Part of Omar dreaded viewing the photographs; part of him had to see them. He examined them with tears in his eyes. Kara sat next to him, put her arm around his shoulders, and cradled his head as he cried.

"Poor Gabrielle. Why her?"

"Omar, I am so sorry."

"I know she is in a better place. But what a wasted life. Thank God I have you. Without you, I might consider joining her." He pointed at the screen, "Look at the bastard. He acts as though nothing happened as he just sneaks off into the afternoon. How does he live with himself even if he didn't push her?"

"Good question. He's a breed apart, that's for sure."

Kara left early. They were both exhausted and tormented. After Kara left, Omar called Louis and asked him to come over. When Louis arrived, Omar showed him the photographs Kara had given him. Louis went very still, and Omar knew that was a dangerous sign.

"Louis, I have a plan for revenge." Omar told him about their scheme to ruin the Senator.

"That's not enough. Gabrielle is dead. How does that compensate for her death?"

Omar regretted sharing the pictures with Louis.

"Louis, let me handle this my way. We don't want another murder on our hands."

"It wouldn't be murder. It would be an execution or if you wish—payment to society for a death that can be repaid only with another death. Like Sebastian."

"No, we can't even consider it. Two wrongs don't make a right. Nothing we do can bring Gabrielle back. Even though he deserves it, we can't justify it."

Louis shrugged his shoulders. *Even the Bible seems to condone a tradeoff; an eye for an eye. . . .*

 ༄

The next few months were filled with wedding plans.

"Omar, I want to get married in Madrid where my family lives."

"Whatever your heart desires, I really don't care if a witch doctor performs the ceremony as long as we're married."

"H-u-m-m, that's an interesting thought. Witch doctor?"

"You wouldn't dare—would you?"

"Of course not, mother would skin me alive."

"And that's the only reason?"

They both laughed.

Kara took a trip home so that she and her parents could firm up the wedding plans. Kara wanted a spring wedding when all of Spain would be awakening from the drab winter and blossoming with new life. So it was settled. The wedding would take place the first day of May.

Kara's mother said, "Kara, let me handle the details. All you have to do is buy the most fabulous wedding dress on planet earth. After all, you are our only child. I will do the rest, including engaging the wedding party. What color do you want the bridesmaids to wear, and do you want Rosa to be your maid of honor?"

"Rosa, absolutely. You pick the colors—you've always had good taste, so I relinquish all the planning to your expertise. And, Mommy, would you invite the Santa Cruzes including Marie. I want to reconcile our differences if she is willing."

Louisa Isabella arched her eyebrows. *Now I'm Mommy, not Mother. I like it! This is out of character. Since when has she appreciated my good taste? And reconciling with Marie, what has happened to our little girl?*

There was no doubt that Mark had the election in his hip pocket. The polls showed he had an overwhelming majority. The fact that he hadn't heard from the blackmailer or Kara in months ceased to bother him. He was on an emotional high, and he thought nothing could spoil his euphoria. His phone rang one night as he sat watching the news and basking in his popularity.

"Hello."

"Is this Mark Langford?"

"Yes."

"You're *done* you lying son-of-a-bitch. Did you kill that girl?"

"What?" The hair rose on Mark's neck. *What the hell now?*

"The picture on the cover of *Hot Pursuit.*"

"What picture, of what?"

"Why don't you drag your sorry ass out and buy a copy," the caller said and slammed down the phone.

Mark dropped the receiver back into its cradle. He jumped up, awkwardly plunged his feet into his shoes, grabbed his coat, and headed for the door. Still jamming his arms into his coat sleeves, he opened the door. As he did so, Louis and Herc pushed their way in, albeit without the ski masks this time but still wearing the black leather gloves.

"Wh . . .wh . . .what do you want. . ?" Mark stuttered, trying to stifle back his fear.

Louis held a copy of the weekly rag, *Hot Pursuit*, in Mark's face. On the cover was a picture

of Mark peering over the balcony as Gabrielle lay
on the pavement in front of the Brookline Apartments. Mark gasped; he didn't know the picture
existed. A foggy remnant of the blackmail scam
crossed his mind, but he was too frightened to try
connecting any dots at that moment. Herc put his
hand on Mark's chest and pushed him back into
the apartment followed by Louis. Louis gingerly
threw his copy of *Hot Pursuit* onto the coffee table.
Mark again glanced at it and grimaced. His heart
began racing as his fear mounted. The telephone
began ringing again. Herc glanced at Louis. He
grabbed the telephone cord and gave it a jerk, dis-
connecting the phone from the wall.

"What are you going . . ," Mark stopped in
mid-sentence when Herc walked over to the glass
doors that led out onto the balcony. He violently
slid them open. A cold November wind ruffled
the magazine and Mark sensed what was going
to happen. Looking at Louis, he murmured, "But,
I thought…"

"Changed my mind," Louis said and nodded
to Herc.

Herc grabbed Mark's upper left arm in a
vice-grip, and Louis grabbed his right one. Mark
offered little resistance as they escorted him out
onto the balcony, his feet barely touching the floor.
Mark had not tied his shoes in his rush to get a
copy of *Hot Pursuit*. One of his shoes came off as
he was dragged across the sliding door track.

Mark looked over at the railing and cried,
"Wait! I'm going to be President, I can . . ."

"What? Can you bring Gabrielle back? I don't think so," Louis hissed.

Mark knew this was the end of the line and, just as he had always heard, his life passed in review behind his closed eyelids, including the White House dream that would never be fulfilled. He whimpered as he whispered a prayer just before the killers each grabbed one of his legs and flung him out into space—twelve stories above the pavement.

The next day, the wire service contained the following story:

MARK LANGFORD PLUNGES TO HIS DEATH

Mark Langford, front-runner presidential candidate, plunged to his death Saturday morning, apparently jumping twelve stories from the balcony of his DC apartment.

Langford was the projected winner as early polls placed him in the lead by an overwhelming majority. The suicide occurred after an article headlined in yesterday's edition of Hot Pursuit.

The story contained a photograph depicting Langford peering over the balcony immediately after beauty queen, Gabrielle LaTana, fell to her death earlier this year. The source of the picture has not been determined. However, Hot Pursuit *stands behind its authenticity.*

Langford's death leaves the Democratic Party without a presidential candidate. Langford's office announced that his remains will be returned to Indianapolis where he maintained a home. Relatives say they will hold a private memorial service. Interment will be at St. Joseph's Cemetery in Carmel, Indiana.

VERN SIMSON SAT with his feet on his desk smoking a stogie when he saw the article about Langford's death in the paper. His first reaction was that he hoped Cynthia saw it as well. That should set that little girl free from her demons. He would have called her, but she covered her tracks so well even he couldn't find her

Cynthia was in the student union building at Loyola when she saw the front page headlines of an abandoned newspaper carelessly tossed on one of the side tables. She dropped her books and collapsed onto the worn, lumpy sofa adjacent the table. She grabbed the paper and read the entire article. Then she reread it. Cynthia slowly absorbed the implications and breathed a sigh of relief. The nightmare was over. *I should feel remorse over the death of a fellow human, but he made my life miserable and, God forgive me, I can't help the way I feel. I've been living in fear and constantly looking over my shoulder. I don't believe he actually jumped—he wouldn't have had the guts.* Picking up her belongings, she stood, her body feeling almost weightless. She experienced the joy and freedom of what she imagined must be tantamount to being released from a prison sentence.

✎

Detective Steve Carson slumped over his desk and studied the open file on Gabrielle LaTana, the *Hot Pursuit* article, and the newspaper headlines proclaiming the death of Senator Mark Langford. Although Langford's death was classified as a suicide, Carson wasn't buying it. *I'm baffled by the phone having been torn from the wall, the untied shoe lying on the balcony, and the fact that the deceased was wearing his overcoat when he jumped and, especially, how far from the building the body landed. That just doesn't fit the suicide theory. Why would a suicidal man hurriedly put on his shoes and coat to jump to his death?*

Carson sat for some minutes fingering the three items; finally he folded the newspapers and inserted them into LaTana's file. Rising, he put the file in a cabinet marked CLOSED CASES. *Maybe justice had been done or perhaps overdone.* He jerked his tweed jacket from the back of his chair, picked up his badge, attached it to his belt, and walked out of the bureau into the soft rain that had been falling all day. Turning his face upward, he let the cool drops refresh his flesh and his spirit before he made a mad dash for his car.

✎

Held on the massive front lawn, Kara and Omar's wedding reception transformed into the quintessential fairytale, made more believable by *Casa de Isabella* as a backdrop. The Isabella estate was groomed for the occasion, and everything was primed for the event. The weather could not have been more cooperative. The flowers, the fountains, the trees, and even the birds were on their best behavior. Round tables with colored canopies were strategically placed so that all the attendees had a view of the raised platform erected for the cake cutting and the traditional tossing of the bridal bouquet. The actual ceremony was held at Holy Trinity Catholic Church in Madrid, but the reception was the showcase of the event. All of the three thousand invited guests attended and brought someone with them or so it appeared to Louisa as the food vanished almost as soon as it was brought out. The music was exuberant, the food was extraordinary, and the wine was exceptional. It would have been sacrilegious to compare the event to the Wedding Feast at Cana but . . . .

"I've had little experience in this line of work," Kara said as they jointly held the cake knife poised above the wedding cake.

"Nor have I," Omar replied. Then surprising Kara, he took control of the situation and plunged the knife deep into the second layer.

"Nice incision, you should have been a surgeon," Kara teased, transferring the mangled piece of cake onto a dessert plate and offering Omar the first bite.

Omar licked his lips and rolled his eyes in ecstasy, indicating the cake was indeed delicious, and after brushing crumbs from his mouth, he took the slice of cake and held it to Kara's lips.

Much to the delight of the guests, albeit to the horror of her mother, Kara abandoned protocol and facetiously took as large a bite as possible. Then, laughing and trying not to spew cake all over, she bent Omar's arm up and crammed the rest of the slice into his mouth, smearing his mustache with frosting. Kara heard him mutter through a mouthful of cake, "You little vixen, I'll get you for that," so she replied, "I hope so, I certainly hope so." The wedding guests howled with glee and clapped in appreciation at the sudden and unexpected frivolity. Joining hands, Kara curtsied and Omar bowed to their fans, and then they each took a napkin and dabbed at each other's mouth until they were once again presentable.

Before turning the serving of the cake over to the servants, Omar cut another slice and placed it on one of the bone-china dessert plates. A surprised Kara stared as he gingerly jumped off the platform and approached his grandmother, who was seated at a table with other relatives. Startled, his grandmother looked up as Omar went down on one knee before her. He placed the slice of cake in front of her, took her hand in his, and gently kissed it. Then, bending close so no one else could hear, he whispered "Mamasetta." His grandmother's frail and bony hand went immediately to the gold cross hanging around her neck. The one Gabrielle had given her years ago. She was moved to tears as she clutched Omar's hand. She finally managed to say, "Be happy, my son. I know Gabrielle is with Tomas and Michelle, and they are all looking down from heaven and blessing this event." Omar, close to tears himself, nodded in agreement.

After the ceremonies: tossing the bridal bouquet; toasting the newlyweds; cake cutting, and first dance, Marie Santa Cruz sought Kara out and pulled her aside. She hugged her and wished her every happiness. Kara returned the hug.

"You know," Kara said. "I've always respected you. You were my only formidable adversary, and you kept me on my toes. If it hadn't been for you, I may not have even made it through school much less with honors. Couldn't let you get ahead of me."

Both girls laughed and Marie volleyed back. "Every so often I get a twinge of pain in my nose and remember the day you broke it. My hate for you spurred me on to great things. I'm now a defense attorney and, I dare say, a damn good one. If you ever get in a jam, give me a call."

"Sure! So you can trip the switch after they strap me in the chair?" Kara raised her eyebrows in dramatic effect and smiled broadly. "Omar and I will be living in Monaco, so if you ever want to visit, you're always welcome. I'd love to show you my estate, so you can eat your heart out."

"Deal! But don't count on me eating my heart out. Remember Don la Salle? Hold on, don't take another swing at me but we're engaged. He finally grew up and made something of himself. He has his own law firm and is doing extremely well. In fact, I work there but he understands I work with him, not *for* him. And I'll bet our estate is far greater than yours—that is, of course, when we get one."

The good-natured bantering between the two allowed them to bond. Kara had desperately needed Marie to forgive her, and it appeared as though she had.

Standing there with newfound respect for each other, they paused and listened to the riotous partygoers as they dined, drank, and danced to the lively music at the reception. Turning, Marie helped Kara gather the skirt of her voluminous gown, and the girls walked back to join in the gaiety. Don approached and took Marie's hand.

"May I have the pleasure of this dance?" he asked, entwining his fingers into Marie's. Don nodded to Kara but his eyes were only for Marie, who effortlessly slipped into his embrace. As they gracefully joined the other dancers, Marie looked back at Kara and winked. Kara thought, *Good for them, I wish them the very best!*

Kara scanned the guests, searching for Omar. Honing in on him as he chatted with Ambassador Madrid, Kara was caught up in the rapture of pure love. At that moment, she was the happiest woman in the world. She suddenly remembered her eighth birthday and Aunt Sophie's prediction, *"Kara, my child, on this your eighth birthday, the stars tell me your future husband will be a very handsome, wealthy, influential man. He will sweep you off your feet, and you will melt in his arms. You will live in a faraway land and find happiness beyond your wildest imagination."* Thank you, Aunt Sophie, wish you could have lived to see this day. . .

ABOUT THE AUTHOR

Judith Blevins has spent her entire professional life experiencing the mystery, intrigue and courtroom drama that unfolds daily within the criminal justice system. Her previous experience as a court clerk, then serving five consecutive district attorneys in Grand Junction, Colorado, has provided the inspiration for her stories. Her second novel, *Swan Song*, is a riveting page-turner that holds the reader in excited anticipation.